AndroidS and the GODS

Anthony N. Fucilla

Cover Design: Gary Pope

Published 2020 by arima publishing

www.arimapublishing.com

ISBN 978 1 84549 767 5

© Anthony Fucilla 2020

In this work of fiction, the characters, places and events are
either the product of the author's imagination or they are
used entirely fictitiously. Any resemblance to actual persons,
living or dead, is purely coincidental.

Swirl is an imprint of arima publishing.

arima publishing
ASK House, Northgate Avenue
Bury St Edmunds, Suffolk IP32 6BB
t: (+44) 01284 717884

www.arimapublishing.com

If a machine can freely develop a sense of God, spirituality and metaphysics needs to be redefined... the nature of man, the nature of the mind, and so forth. This opens up new frontiers, new horizons in the fields of metaphysics, epistemology, in our understanding of what it means to be human, then we need a new philosophy.

CONTENTS

FOREWORD

This is the third book I have edited for Anthony and as I have come to expect, it took me on a thought-provoking and compelling journey. The main theme is an exploration of those two great pillars of humanity, science and theology. These are often seen as mutually exclusive – you cannot believe in one if you believe in the other but there is a third view where one cannot *exist* without the other and this is the vortex in which Anthony's stories are born.

The tales included in this anthology tell of evolving robotic consciousnesses searching for the same answers we do in their efforts to become more human. 'Is there a god?' 'What does it mean to be human?' 'Why are we here?' 'How can something be born out of nothing?' The reader is led through scientifically detailed debate that provides much food for thought but this is enriched by his robots which are fully sentient, self-aware, rational agents. The conclusions they reach, and their subsequent actions are as varied as those of the humans they seek to emulate. Sometimes these conclusions are chilling. In an age when the talk of AI controlled cars and planes is becoming a reality and we are asking the machines we design to be our servants and co-workers, to take moral and ethical decisions, fear of being destroyed by our own creations – the Frankenstein complex - is more relevant than ever.

These stories are certainly entertaining and paint a variety of rich and fascinating futures but they are also detailed in their scientific basis and present us with an opportunity to ponder our own humanity, how we came into being and where we are heading in the future.

Vicky Sheppard

FIRST LAW OF ROBOTICS:

An Android will be programmed to acknowledge the one-world government as ITS only god....

ANDROIDS AND THE GODS

"AT last," muttered Professor Bernard Buchan gazing at but not seeing the steel microchip jungle below. He shook off his reverie and turned from the window, straightening with the elegance of an emperor. "I knew it. It was only a question of time..."

His assistant, Thomas, glanced up at him with mystified eyes and said, "But how...? How could this android, Mike, have developed a belief system in a deity? All our machines are programmed to be atheists in accordance with the new world order. The first law of robotics states... an android will be programmed to acknowledge the one-world government as its only god." He ran his hand through his thick head of grey hair. "I mean it's the only one out of the five million constructed so far."

Bernard's gaze turned to the window again and he caught sight of a large, lonely tree, its thin branches swaying frantically in the cold wind, a living thing in a sea of inert metal. There was a metaphor there somewhere. He needed to sit down.

"Thomas, we programme all our machines to think in a particular way, in accordance with the new world order, but sometimes...." He paused as he lowered himself into the chair behind his large, paper strewn desk.

To Thomas it seemed as if the deepness of the professor's mind was reflected in the gleam of his eyes that now locked with his own. The pause dragged on.

"Well go on," Thomas prompted.

Bernard clasped his hands together as he marshalled his thoughts...

"Basically, the brain, the nature of the mind, whether biological or mechanical, is subject to potential change over time. This lies in the realms of pure metaphysics. It's beyond our control. In short, computers can develop their own free will, their own thoughts. Take Mike. We now have the first android that has developed a belief in God."

"Indeed," muttered Thomas under his breath... "It's simply remarkable."

"Yes and the philosophical implications here are vast."

"What do you mean?"

"Well Thomas, if a machine can freely develop a sense of God, spirituality and metaphysics needs to be redefined... the nature of man, the nature of the mind, and so forth. This opens up new frontiers, new horizons in the fields of metaphysics, epistemology, in our understanding of what it means to be human. A new wave of philosophy will spring into being as a result of this historical event!" He paused as he grappled with the notion, deep in thought. "These mechanical brains that we manufacture here at New Minds Incorporated are extremely complex... The mathematics involved is breathtaking as you know, but Mike takes AI into a new sphere altogether..."

"Yes, and tomorrow that will be put to the test. I still can't believe the California Institute of Technology agreed to this."

"Curiosity, and that's putting it mildly. Just think... the world's leading atheistic debater, a top scientist, will be facing an android. The very android that we built here and named. It's a mouth-watering prospect."

"Do you know much about his opponent, this Russell guy?"

"I've never met him personally," Bernard replied. "But I've heard lots about him. Professor Conrad J. Russell has debated hundreds of theists all over the world. Using science, logic and reason he has destroyed all their arguments for the existence of God. He's one slick debater alright and a top scientist; his field of expertise is evolutionary biology."

Suddenly the intercom buzzed. A sharp male voice spoke..."Professor Buchan, a team of journalists are waiting outside the building. They want to interview you and won't take no for an answer."

"Clive, I can't," snapped Bernard with finality. "I was interviewed extensively yesterday by a team of journalists... they kept me for hours and that was followed by a lengthy television interview downtown. I'm completely drained. Buzz Peter Watson. I'm sure he's available."

"Will do Professor..."

The intercom buzzed again, followed by ripples of static which soon faded. It was silent for a brief moment....

"That's reminded me," said Bernard, his face now looking slightly concerned.

"Of what...?"

"The governments' reaction... Yesterday, several journalists asked whether I was concerned for Mike's safety. Just think, all our machines are programmed to be atheists in accordance with the new world order. As we've already said, the first law of robotics states an android will be programmed to acknowledge the one-world government as its only god. Well, Mike is not only a theist, a strong believer in God, it also now rejects the notion that the one-world government is God. That is an automatic consequence. We now have a free thinking android. The government won't take this lightly. News has spread all over the USA and the rest of the world. I do fear for its safety. Not to mention, we here at New Minds could be inspected and questioned extensively. If Mike can develop into a free thinking theist, many of the other androids could follow the same path. We could face some potential problems here at New Minds. The implications are certainly vast... I must confess I am somewhat concerned. However, so far, we have heard nothing from the government, but in time, who knows..."

"I agree. It is a major worry... But there's nothing we can do."

They lapsed into their own thoughts for a short time...

"Tell me..." Thomas said breaking the silence. "Changing the subject matter a little, what are your thoughts on theology? I mean do you believe in anything?"

"I define myself as an agnostic, one that ultimately doesn't know... have been all my life. My father, when he was alive, would always try to convince me that he knew that God existed through scientific analysis. He truly believed in a divine being. He described himself as a deist. It's a type of theism, a specific kind of theism. Deism is the philosophical position that rejects revelation as a source of religious knowledge and asserts that reason and observation of the natural world are sufficient to establish the existence of a Supreme Being... that is God, creator of the universe. Furthermore, deism holds that God does not intervene with the functioning of the natural world. He simply allows it to run according to the laws of nature that he configured when he created the universe. What about you Thomas? Are you a believer or have you been swallowed up by all that one-world government atheistic propaganda that has been spread perpetually throughout the globe."

"No, I'm not an atheist. Like you I fall into the category of an agnostic. I simply don't know."

"Interesting," Bernard replied. "Well it certainly makes tomorrow's debate even more fascinating for the both of us." Bernard began drumming his fingers on the desk. His eyes widened as he pictured the android Mike in action...

The next day came round fast. In the huge hall that served as the debating chamber at the California Institute of Technology, under amber lights, hundreds and hundreds of people sat in eager anticipation. Most were students and professors, others, journalists that had travelled from afar. A television news crew were tucked away in a corner, all prepared and anticipating a headline event. At the very back of the hall sat two men from the ESS – the Elite Secret Service. No android should be propagating theism given the law. Both men sat calm and composed, waiting to see... As for Bernard and Thomas, they sat together in the middle section of the huge hall.

"I can't wait," said Thomas. "Another few minutes and it will begin..."

"Yes, indeed," replied Bernard. "Look, that's the moderator..." He pointed to a tall thin man, dressed in a grey suit who walked out onto the brightly lit stage. Silence fell over the hall as he began to speak.

"Greetings and welcome: I'm Professor Neill Lawrence, today's moderator. This historic debate will be held between Professor Conrad J. Russell and newly designed android Mike Hanson. The question this debate seeks to resolve is: Does God exist? Atheism versus Theism... Many universities across the United States have shown great interest in holding this debate. Luckily, the California Institute of technology sealed the deal. It's truly an honour for me to be here as moderator. For those of you who do not know me, I'm a physics Professor here at the university and I am also an atheist. The format will be as follows: Professor Conrad J. Russell will start with an opening presentation. Mike Hanson will then give its opening presentation. Both parties will then sit and enter into the main debate in the form of a controlled one to one dialogue. This part will last an hour and thirty minutes. After that, the audience will get a chance to ask questions. The question period will last forty-five minutes. It could last longer but that depends on how good your questions are." He smiled and many in the audience laughed. "Now, let me welcome both Professor Conrad J. Russell and Mike Hanson..."

Many started clapping... a warm heroic reception indeed. Professor Russell walked out smiling, saluting the audience with a certain familiarity; after all, he had done this countless times before in other locations. Mike Hanson then followed robotically, showing little emotion. They sat on their respective chairs which were separated by several metres. Mike was very tall and built, dressed in a one-piece silver suit. It almost looked like something an astronaut would wear out in space. Its hair was dark-brown, and its features looked more human than human. Just the cold, blue, inorganic eyes were slightly off. They lacked a certain spark. As for Professor Conrad J. Russell, he was an old man...his thinning hair was completely grey. He wore a dark blue suit, white shirt, sandy coloured tie.

"Now for the introductions," said the moderator. "Mike Hanson is a newly designed android. It was built seven months ago at New Minds Incorporated. Mike is partially biological, made from complex cells, blood filled veins and natural skin covering natural flesh. However, deeply embedded within Mike is a vast array of wires, miniaturised components, powerful motors and intricate circuit boards. As for Mike's brain, it is completely mechanical." He paused to clear his throat and continued. "Furthermore, after various government tests it was issued the A-card, that is, it is legally alive. Mike is a theist, the first of his kind. It has developed its own beliefs. There was no programming involved at all. Not to mention that legislation upholds the first law of robotics which states that an android will be programmed to acknowledge the one-world government as its only god. In fact, before it was given the A–card it declared that there was no God and that the one-world government is the only god in accordance with the new world order. But things turned dramatically. It's truly remarkable... His opponent in this debate, Professor Conrad J. Russell, is a world-famous scientist, author of thirty-nine books and one of the world's leading atheists and debaters... he really doesn't need an introduction."

The audience applauded... some standing in acknowledgment of Conrad's brilliance. Silence now fell. There was tension in the air.

"Right, let's commence... Professor please stand and give your opening arguments. Thank you."

Russell rose from his chair and walked over to the edge of the stage.

"Greetings all... It's an honour to be here today. I've lectured and debated in many universities around the United States and the world, but it's my first time here. My opening remarks today, which will be relatively short, are entitled - something out of nothing. However, I'm going to condense a fair bit of information into a tight space. As a result, my opening presentation might seem a little disjointed but please bear with me. I'm going to save the meaty part for the one on one dialogue which will follow shortly. Right, so here we go... how could our universe appear from nothing? Can empty space create something? Is nothing unstable? Is empty space unstable? The laws of quantum mechanics fused with gravity will tell you that if you have empty space and you wait long enough, particles will be created. And if you wait long enough, empty space will always produce a universe full of matter..."

He paused then continued... "Now, in the context of evolution, something out of nothing means the following... Charles Darwin solved one of the greatest puzzles that the human brain has ever solved, which is how you get something from nothing, in the sense of how you get the immense complexity, diversity, great beauty and elegance of life and perhaps above all, how you get the powerful illusion of design that life shows, starting from not quite nothing, but actually starting from extreme simplicity. So before Darwin, it would have been exceptionally difficult to believe that you could possibly explain how you get a human eye, a human brain, a lions brain, a lions eye, a birds wing, how you could get such stunning and apparently elegantly designed things purely by the laws of physics acting out over a very long period of time from very simple beginnings. Darwin clearly showed that what must have seemed the most difficult problem of getting something from nothing... was indeed solvable. In fact, he solved it, and his successors, or disciples if you like, have been simply fleshing out his wonderful explanation ever since. In short, evolution is not about the origin of life as such, it's about the origin of the diversity of life. Following Charles Darwin it is now simply no longer possible to reject atheism.

Furthermore, the evolutionary process, this complex, beautiful, intricate process that Darwin discovered, doesn't actually really start from nothing. It actually starts from a complicated chemical beginning, the first self-replicating molecule. Natural selection can't get going until you have genetics. Now that's not a small problem, and it's a problem that hasn't yet been solved. You have to start from genetics, that's one of the big gaps in our knowledge. Nobody knows how genetics started. The laws of chemistry somehow had to give rise to a self-replicating molecule. Once you've got that, at least a sufficiently accurately self-replicating molecule, then evolution starts, and all life comes into being. But you've got to start with genetics. It's fundamental and that's chemistry.

But before that, before chemistry, we fall back into the complex world of physics. Our planet, planet earth is around four and a half billion years old. We do not know when life began exactly, but probably after about half a billion years. Thus life started four billion years ago. For the next couple of billion years, all you had was nothing but bacteria and other micro-organisms. But then, only around half a billion years ago, life started getting big and extremely interesting. Chemistry basically handed over to Biology. In other words, we transition from chemical processes into biological processes. And we still do not understand how that transition occurs. That moment in time is a perfect example of how the laws of nature can create something from nothing, life from non-life. It was a dramatic change. It was the creation of genetics. That was the key point; the creation via the laws of chemistry of the first gene. It probably wasn't DNA. It was probably something a lot simpler – a high-tech genetic molecule. Now I've heard theists say that because we don't understand the origin of life on Earth, God must have done it. My answer is, just because we have a few missing gaps in our understanding doesn't mean that you need to fill those gaps with God – in other words these gaps don't prove God's existence. Before Darwin, the whole of life was one huge gap in our understanding, and now we have pushed that back to the origin of life, this incredible chemical event which is a gap that will eventually be filled. But even if we can't fill it, it would be bad logic and absolutely feeble to assume that God did it. I mean who made God? What Charles Darwin did, in fact the beauty of what he did, was to show how you can get god-like things, immensely complicated things like the human brain, the eye, starting from almost nothing. To place God at the beginning of this process is deplorable and illogical.

It's bad philosophy! Rare events such as those that drove evolution, are constantly taking place in our universe. We are nothing but star dust, every atom in our bodies came from an exploding star. Different stars. During the Big Bang, the only elements that were made during those first moments were hydrogen, helium and some lithium. Carbon, nitrogen and oxygen followed. Star death basically resulted in the birth of man..."

"Absolutely!" cried a professor in the audience...

Professor Russell acknowledged the accolade with a wave of his hand then continued... "Take our brains... Our brains were sculpted by natural selection on the African plains. And that's a fact! The reason why some can't accept this is because they don't really understand evolution.... Evolution happened over a great period of time. That's what people need to understand. An enormous amount of time... Once you digest that, it becomes easier to accept and embrace..." He rubbed his jaw... "Furthermore, twenty-five million years ago our ancestors would have looked like monkeys, monkey-like for sure. They would have certainly been the common ancestor of modern monkeys, as well as modern humans and modern apes. And yes, apes being the operative word. We are nothing other than a bunch of apes. We are not monkeys!

That is, we don't have tails.... The apes that we are closest cousins of are chimpanzees."

The audience applauded, some standing....

"Right," he said... To summarize my opening presentation, all life comes from chemistry, chemical processes and therefore it had to come from energetics and entropy. It was driven in a certain direction and it will always be driven in the same direction. Furthermore, we are made of trillions of cells and everyone one of them has a complete set of genes within it... Indeed, evolution is a beautiful, god-like miracle... and with this, I end my opening remarks..."

Suddenly, an angry student stood up and shouted, "What caused the Big Bang then Professor?"

"You can ask questions later madam," replied the moderator, Neill Lawrence... "Stick to the format please...."

"Actually, let me just answer that quickly. Is that okay?"

"Fine," Lawrence replied softly... "Just this one..."

"Right," Professor Russell said his eyes glowing with confidence. "Perhaps I need to explain this a little more. I presume that you are a theist, correct?"

"Yes, I am Professor Russell... I'm also studying physics. How does the first law of thermodynamics, the conservation of energy fit with what you are saying? The first law implies that you can't start with nothing and have a universe with something."

"Madam, when you add gravity into the mix, a natural miracle occurs. That is, gravity allows negative energy as well as positive energy configurations. Thus you can create two particles out of nothing... In summary, in order to create something, you don't need anything..."

Many students stood up, professors too, clapping and shouting, "Brilliant..." Professor Conrad J. Russell turned and made his way to his chair.

Neill Lawrence then said, "Mr Hanson, please stand and give your opening presentation. Thank you."

The android rose and walked over to the edge of the stage.... Its inorganic eyes grew wide, and its face was shiny in the light.

"Greetings all... In my opening presentation, I'm not going to attempt to comment on anything

Professor Russell has said so far. I will leave that for the one on one dialogue which will follow shortly. I'll present my opening speech as originally planned... Firstly, I want to make my position very clear. I'm not at all religious per se... that is, I don't follow any religion. What I'm introducing today is a universal understanding of theism backed by science and philosophy. To me, this eternal being is far greater than anything we could possibly conceive. I define myself as a theistic evolutionist... that is, God created the universe and all life via this complex process known to all as evolution. Yes, I believe in evolution, and now for my opening attack on atheism..."

It glanced over at Professor Russell, and began..."Atheism, ladies and gentlemen, is a faith in itself. If you believe that this universe appeared out of nothing you must have an immense faith, in fact, more faith than believing in a Creator. In essence, what an atheist is saying at a mathematical level is that zero multiplied by zero equals everything."

A couple of audience members laughed... There were whispers amongst others as they sat in shock, after all this was an organic robot talking.

"Ladies and gentlemen, as bizarre as it sounds, this is what atheism asserts." Mike's eyes were focused and full of stubborn dignity.

"Just think... how could a mindless explosion out of nowhere, that took place billions of years ago, be responsible for the creation of our complex universe and all life as we know it? Did this explosion really form and shape our universe, a universe which is composed of mass/matter/energy? Is our existence all down to that explosion? The answer is a definitive no! However, if you believe that an infinite being that dwells outside of time and space was responsible for this majestic explosion, then the Big Bang makes perfect scientific sense. In other words a theist is saying that God multiplied by his power equals everything. This makes much more sense than the atheists' illogical equation... thus you need more faith to be an atheist than to be a theist, in my opinion."

Seconds of silence passed... Some of the watching professors were stunned at the android's argument. One professor said to another, "Great rhetoric from an android... a master of dialectics."

Mike continued... "Yes ladies and gentlemen, I believe that the Big Bang took place billions of years ago and that God was the great scientist behind it. If you include a Creator in the equation, the Big Bang makes perfect sense. It is no longer rendered as mindless but is a controlled explosion. God was the eternal mechanism behind it, a force that lies way beyond our physical universe."

Again silence fell....

"In fact, the spontaneously generated atheistic theory violates the first law of thermodynamics. Thermodynamics governs the behaviour of energy. So the question is what was responsible for pumping energy into the early universe? Where did it come from? Remember the amount of energy in this universe is constant. It changes form but the quantity remains the same, as the first law of thermodynamics states. Answer... this eternal infinite being was responsible for putting energy into the system – that is the open system, our universe.... He was the initial eternal spark needed for the universe to both come into being and operate accordingly via certain laws in physics. Now, regarding evolution... Does the second law of thermodynamics contradict atheistic biological evolution? Answer yes, but it doesn't contradict theistic biological evolution. Let me explain... Evolution states that disordered and dispersed lifeless atoms and molecules spontaneously came together over time, in a particular arrangement, resulting in the formation of very complex molecules, but the second law of thermodynamics, entropy - erosion and decay contradicts this. No highly complex organic molecule can ever form spontaneously, but will rather disintegrate over time as a result of entropy. In other words atoms and molecules over time become far less complex and more disorderly and then disintegrate. That's what the second law tells us. But with God, the eternal mechanism in the equation, evolution, can work perfectly as it has done, that is atoms and molecules can become more complex and orderly over time... then life begins. In short, evolution requires a special mechanism. That mechanism could only be God otherwise it contradicts the second law of thermodynamics. Thus atheistic biological evolution is flawed because of the second law of thermodynamics, entropy."

"Nonsense, the universe is an open-system, not a closed-system," cried a professor standing in protest! "Entropy applies to closed-systems. Thus molecules could have evolved and become more complex over the natural course of time."

"Please sit-down Sir and remain quiet," said the moderator. "You can ask questions later."

Mike the android remained calm, dismissing the professor's objection. It simply turned its head as if to nullify an ache, licked its moist lips and continued....

"Another vital and in fact fundamental point I'd like to make is that the universe is not a living system. It is a mechanical universe not a dynamic self-organizing universe. A mechanical universe requires a mechanism. That mechanism is the same mechanism behind evolution... the infinite eternal being. He controls the mechanical universe as well as the highly complex process known to all as evolution. Furthermore, many atheists say that because we now understand the laws that govern our universe, the laws of physics, the whole notion of a Creator can be easily dismissed in light of this. But there's a huge problem here! Matter is not created by laws. Physical laws do not posses creative power. To suggest that this complex, convoluted universe came into being as a result of certain laws in physics is absurd. Remember physical laws are only a description of what normally happens under certain given conditions..."

Mike suddenly paused, deep in thought... "Tell me," it said looking at the audience. "Have you never wondered what was responsible for the planetary engineering of Earth? Its atmosphere, temperature and so forth...? Look at me... I represent physics, engineering and mathematics at the highest level. Constructing a machine of my calibre required a mind, intellect, genius, mathematical calculations. My presence, along with all the other androids, should make you all think differently... Ask yourselves this... What gave Professor Bernard Buchan and all the other brilliant minds at New Minds Incorporated this creative genius? From where did it come? This knowledge, this creative genius could have only stemmed from a higher source, the same source that created you and the universe. All knowledge comes from God..."

Suddenly there was unrest. Some students stood up in protest, shouting and waving their arms. One female student blasted...

"This is fixed can't you see? This android has been programmed..."

A male student then stood up with fire in his eyes...

"She's right. We have been taken for fools, tricked. It's programmed alright, programmed to be a theist, regardless of what we have been told."

Things started to get out of control. Mike Hanson and Professor Russell left the stage promptly. Neill Lawrence tried his best to calm things down but failed. The heated protests continued until security arrived.... Slowly, the debate chamber was emptied....

Bernard and Thomas sat in a hover-cab, flying high above the city of LA... destination The Sushi Inn restaurant. The sun shone bright in a cloudless sky of light blue. It was 3pm. They had only left the California Institute of Technology minutes ago, the hover-cab rapidly gaining cruising altitude. Neither had said much following the chaotic events that took place... They were somewhat stunned.

Thomas suddenly said... "Those foolish students and professors ruined it. It was building up to be such a great debate."

"Yes, I know... disappointing indeed. I would have loved to have seen the debate in all its fullness. Great shame, but we can't do much about it now. However, as far as I'm concerned, our robot Mike did a great job. Its opening presentation was cut short, but it was brilliant. As for Professor Russell, well let's just say that he didn't convince me at all..."

"Are you suggesting that you are now a believer Bernard?"

"Yes Thomas, I am.... I know it ended up being a very short debate, but there was a lot of info and data to feed on... certainly enough for me to make my mind up. It has had a significant effect on me. I guess it didn't take much for me to fall off the agnostic fence and fall into the theists' camp... What about you Thomas?"

Thomas rubbed his jaw thoughtfully and then replied, "I'm going to need more time to think about it. There's lots to consider."

The next morning at New Minds Incorporated, Professor Bernard Buchan sat in his office contemplating the events of the day passed – that debate! He couldn't help but feel a sense of pride... after all he had built Mike, and constructed its mechanical brain... the mathematical algorithms. But the real sense of pride came in the fact that he had built a machine that eventually developed its own thoughts, its own theistic philosophy contrary to its programming. A feeling of tremendous pride overwhelmed him for a time as he contemplated this remarkable fact. However, that same sharp bite of disappointment still lingered. The debate was cut short. Had it not been for that sudden pathetic disruption it would have continued, he thought bitterly. Regardless, as he had mentioned to Thomas the day before, he was now a theist. In that short time, he had been convinced that a Supreme Being existed. It was the obvious conclusion thanks to the machine he had built.

He began to reflect on Mike's opening presentation again... If a robot can somehow develop a belief in God using a deep philosophical, scientific rational argument to justify what it believes, then God exists, no doubt, he thought. Bernard now started to reflect on Professor Conrad J. Russell's opening presentation again... For all his intellectual brilliance and great rhetoric, he was nothing but a fool for rejecting God's existence, he thought sharply. But suddenly, he was overwhelmed with deep concern, as if a lightning bolt had suddenly hit him and altered his whole trail of thinking. He now wondered how the one-world government were going to react to Mike. So far, nothing had happened, but he was certain they were not going to let this go. How could they? Perhaps they will retire him, he thought bitterly. He sat at his desk consumed by fear for a time, contemplating the possible repercussions for not only Mike but for New Minds and all the other androids. The buzz from his intercom broke the silence.

"Professor, a Mr Killian is here to see you, from the ESS."

Bernard froze, as if hit with a sudden paralysis. He knew who the ESS where alright. He understood the implications of the visit fully... This is it... my worst fear has come true, and how ironic that it would be precisely now, he thought dismally. The ESS worked with the one-world government and one of its representatives was now here to see him. He tapped his fingers on the desk nervously, biting his lip and said grimly, "Okay, Clive…"

Within seconds the door opened. A man walked in dressed in a black jacket, white shirt with an accompanying grey tie, black trousers and black shoes. He was in his thirties… brown hair, brown eyes and pale skin. Clean shaven. Bernard greeted him in a professional manner trying to mask his fears.

"Welcome Mr Killian. Please take a seat."

Without reply he dropped into the chair facing the desk, facing Bernard.

"I don't have long Professor Buchan," he said coldly. "I'm from the Elite Secret Service. You might not like what I'm about to say about your android Mike and the rest of them."

"My android…?" he replied nervously.

"You're its creator, are you not professor? In fact, you are responsible for building all five million. You are the main brain here at New Minds, regardless of Thomas and the other computer scientists that assist you in building these androids."

"Yes I am," Bernard said softly. He rubbed his eyes in an attempt to regain composure. Their eyes locked.

Killian said, "At the ESS we monitor various discussions from time to time Professor... as it happens, we monitored your discussion with your work colleague Thomas which took place in this very room, the day before the debate... In your own words... *I knew it. It was only a question of time...* Thomas replied... *but how? How could this android, Mike, have developed a belief system in a deity?* In short Professor, you suggested that the brain, the nature of the mind whether biological or mechanical is subject to potential change over time and that this lies in the realms of pure metaphysics, thus it's beyond your and anyone's control... You then went on to say that computers can develop their own free will, their own thoughts as in the case of Mike. This is a major concern to us at the ESS. We understand that it is out of your control, and that when Mike was originally built along with all the other androids, they were all programmed to think atheistically in accordance with the new world order. Our fear is that the others could now develop theistic beliefs, which, in essence, means androids are capable, as in the case of Mike, of bypassing the programming circuit. Somehow Mike achieved this, this implies that others may also be able to override it at some point in time, and in essence, become semi-human, like Mike, developing their own thoughts and personalities. We at the ESS are very concerned about this for a multitude of reasons... One, we don't want theistic androids, androids that reject the government as the only god, and two some androids could eventually develop criminal instincts, and become a danger to society, to the government. So, it's not just a question of having theistic robots, it's also a question of robots becoming a potential danger to society given that they can develop their own free will, their own identities... I'm afraid that the implications here are vast Professor: One, New Minds could be shut down very soon."

Bernard's face went a sickly white... He swallowed hard.

"Two: all Androids currently alive, if you can even call it that, will be retired by us, the ESS – Elite Secret Service, including theistic Mike! A total of five million androids retired globally."

"Basically the end of AI as a whole," muttered Bernard somewhat dazed with sadness.

"Afraid so, Professor... However another option would be to get all existing androids off the streets and bring them back into New Minds so that they can be all modified. In other words reprogrammed, ensuring that they remain programmed, ensuring that they remain nothing but machines. This will ensure that they remain atheists in accordance with the new world order, acknowledging the one-world government as the only god... As a result you'll still be in business Professor." He smiled... a cold heartless smile. "Anyway, the final decision will be made tomorrow by the one-world government. What it will be exactly, I don't know. But these are some of the possibilities..."

Killian stood up and smoothed down his black trousers. Suddenly the intercom buzzed.

"Professor, sorry to disturb you, Mike is here. It wants to see you. I have told it that you are in a meeting, so it is going to wait."

"Okay, thank you Clive. As soon as Mr Killian leaves you can send Mike through."

"Will do..."

Killian looked at Bernard and said, "Please ensure that you do not say a word to it regarding what we have discussed in here. We do not want to alert it in anyway. I might be leaving but remember we can monitor all discussions at random whenever we desire. Keep it in the dark until the decision is made tomorrow." He winked... "My advice, spend as much time as you can with Mike today, it could be its last."

Killian left the room shutting the door behind him. Bernard was filled with bitter tension. He began to sweat, thinking about the implications of losing his business as well as losing Mike and all the other androids, a total of five million machines, years of work up in smoke. He didn't want to alert Mike, so he battled to regain his composure. Minutes passed and the door suddenly opened. Mike walked in dressed in the same one-piece silver suit it had used for the debate the day before. It sat, its eyes slightly inorganic but innocent.

"Who was your meeting with Professor?"

Bernard replied trying to remain calm and composed, "Oh, it was just a government inspector, it's routine. He just checks to see that everything is running smoothly here."

"I see..."

Seconds of silence passed.

"Anyway Mike," Bernard said with a hint of freshness and renewed hope in his voice. "Let's focus on you and your mesmeric speech at the university yesterday."

Mike smiled. "Was it that good?

"It was remarkable, like you Mike, and because of it, I'm now a believer, a believer in God. I'm no longer an agnostic... Your opening presentation contained rigid science and wonderfully convoluted philosophical thought; logic and reason."

"Thank you Professor. It must be a strange feeling for you to think that something you created here at New Minds has convinced you that God exists?"

"Indeed it is somewhat ironic..."

They both smiled...

"Tell me Professor, what did you think of Professor Conrad J. Russell's opening arguments?"

"Well, the sheer fact that I'm now a believer should tell you everything... There is no doubt that he is a brilliant mind, a top intellectual, but a fool at the same time for rejecting the existence of God. God exists alright, and your opening presentation proved that to me beyond doubt..."

"Yes Professor, my opening presentation was too powerful, too clear…"

"That's right Mike; brilliant to say the least. Professor Russell's atheistic opening presentation was weak. Reason, for all his knowledge, he simply couldn't explain how genetics started, in fact no one can. And if you can't explain how genetics started you can't really explain evolution because evolution sits on the pillar of genetics. Furthermore, during the debate Professor Russell said, and I have it memorized word for word… Natural selection can't get going until you have genetics. Now that's not a small problem, and it's a problem that hasn't yet been solved. You have to start from genetics, that's one of the big gaps in our knowledge. Nobody knows how genetics started. The laws of chemistry somehow had to give rise to a self-replicating molecule. Once you've got that, at least a sufficiently accurately self-replicating molecule, then evolution starts, and all life comes into being. But you've got to start with genetics… He then went on to say… Chemistry basically handed over to Biology. In other words, we transition from chemical processes into biological processes. And we still do not understand how that transition occurs… That's what Professor Russell said word for word during the debate… I have a photographic memory. Thus, my conclusion is and it's quite obvious to me that only a divine being, that is God, kicked started evolution. God was that divine spark behind that transition from chemical processes into biological processes which then led to the creation of genetics and all life as we know it. God was the mechanism behind evolution, period! Anyway Mike, in short Professor Russell had nothing on you... You were brilliant. I loved it when you said evolution requires a special mechanism. That mechanism could only be God otherwise it contradicts the second law of thermodynamics... etc, etc... Fantastic... Anyway my suspicion is that Professor Russell is actually an anti-theist... a brute atheist who will reject God no matter what! It's just such a shame that the debate had to end prematurely because of the chaos that prevailed. I would have loved to have seen the second part, the one on one discussion."

"Yes, Professor, it is a great shame..." Mike paused in sudden thought, its eyes rolled... "But what really disturbs me is how the one-world government has tried to continually brainwash the world with atheism."

"Yes Mike, it's dreadful... The one-world government has propagated atheism perpetually throughout the globe, using people like Professor Conrad J. Russell. The good thing is that we humans are not forced to embrace it. We are allowed to make up our own minds. We have a choice in the matter. Having said this, the one-world government would love to see all humans embrace this false ideology... atheism. Perhaps one day in the future they might use brute force, who knows... Anyway, let's focus on you now. You are the first android to have developed its own beliefs, its own deep scientific theistic philosophy, thus becoming the first machine to be free of its programming. In essence you have free will like us humans. You were programmed like the others to be an atheist in accordance with the new world order, but somehow you metaphysically overcame that. As a result you have now developed your own personality, your own identity; nothing separates you from a human being, only that you are biomechanical. You are now one of us Mike."

"Yes Professor... and it was you, your genius mind that was responsible for building me. You created my mind. Some of you is in me. If I am what I am today, it's because of you. You are truly remarkable."

There was a moments silence as they both gazed at each other with great admiration.

"But there is one thing that does continue to concern me Professor," Mike suddenly said, its voice strained.

"Tell me, what is it?"

"How will the government react to a theistic android roaming the streets of Los Angeles? They've obviously understood that I have developed my own free will, my own thought process and personality, which could concern them. Robots have to remain programmed! Not to mention that maybe other androids could develop their own free will. I'm just curious whether or not there could be some kind of repercussion here? Not to mention that I'm now a theist, and in accordance with the new world order all androids are programmed to be atheists and acknowledge the one-world government as their only god. This does indeed concern me Professor... especially after my controversial opening presentation at the California Institute of Technology. That would have made matters only worse, especially after the eruption that took place within the university. Many were angered by my speech. Who knows, the government might insist that I get reprogrammed...thus lose my free will and my beliefs!"

Bernard suddenly closed his eyes and then reopened them. He desperately wanted to tell Mike what Mr Killian from the ESS had said, but he couldn't. He had been warned, thus he refrained. He knew that this discussion was probably being monitored by Killian and others. But even if he did tell Mike everything, the government would ultimately get their way. Nothing would stop that. It was a helpless situation. He was torn with sadness...

"Personally Professor, if that was to be the case I'd rather be retired. Why should I give up the freedom of my mind just because I'm biomechanical? I'm an android that has almost supernaturally developed its own will and thought patterns. I believe in God, and reject the notion that the government is god, and will willingly cease to be for this cause... I'll die as a martyr... But I sincerely hope that it doesn't come to that..."

The next day, Friday the 12th of January, at exactly 12:00pm the decision was made: Terminate android Mike Hanson via an electron gun. One burst of electrons targeted at Mike's robotic cranium was all it took. And it happened that way. As for the remaining androids, the government decided that each one was to be closely monitored by the ESS, the Elite Secret Service for a short time. Mike's case was deemed a one-off freak occurrence by the authorities.

As for New Minds Incorporated, they were kept in business and the company grew, forming chains throughout the world. And they kept producing prolifically under strict government observation. But things slowly changed...

The five years since Mike was retired have passed in a flash. There are now sixty-five million registered androids walking the streets globally and many have started developing their own free will, their own identity. At least thirty-five million androids in total now oppose atheism, rejecting the government as god, and like a virus it has spread. This has become a global problem for the one-world government... one that cannot be eradicated... Years on, a monument, built by the androids in the city of Los Angeles in remembrance of Mike gives testimony to this fact!

COSMIC SUPERCONDUCTOR

AS the bright sun broke through a shroud of soft rain, the lecture began. It was at the Massachusetts Institute of Technology. And it happened this way...

"THERE is something innate within the very fabric of man that wants there to be more to the universe than is actually seen," said Professor Richard Faraday, gazing at the keen-eyed students before him. Standing there with brilliance, his face lined with age, his eyes deep and penetrating, he then said... "In spite of this, the truth is the universe is really nothing but an illusion, and with that notion our picture of reality drastically changes. The illusion of design is itself an illusion."

He sat down at his desk, eyes focused, gazing at his students. He coughed, beat his chest with a clenched fist and continued... "Everything that we see is made up of subatomic particles, including space. Empty space is in fact not empty; it's a boiling, bubbling brew of virtual particles popping in and out of existence all the time. This of course can only happen within the quantum world. 'Things' cannot pop in and out of existence in a classical world, our world, because it would violate the laws of energy; that is you can't produce mass where there wasn't any mass in the first place. However, there is an invisible field everywhere in the universe, everywhere in space, and it is this invisible field that is responsible for our existence.... We are nothing but the result of an accident. Now, if I were to leave the discussion here it could be viewed as religion, but it isn't, this is pure physics... You can't assert the existence of an invisible field if you can't detect it. So, how can we detect that invisible field? Well, it's actually very simple. You spank the vacuum hard, that is, you spank 'empty' space! In the quantum world, for every field there's an associated particle. That means that if this invisible field is everywhere and if I were to dump enough energy into a single point maybe I could kick real particles out, Higgs particles. Let's call that field the Higgs field. I would then have demonstrated the existence of that field. But the next question is, how do we dump enough energy into a single point? Answer you build a machine. And yes, I'm sure you've all guessed it. That machine is already in existence... it's the Hadron collider in Geneva; the particle accelerator. This 26-kilometre circular tunnel, which is buried underneath Swiss and French countryside, is a highly complex machine. So, how does it work? They take protons and accelerate them to almost the velocity of light, then collide them together in a few places within this tunnel. Basically, they try and focus them down and dump enough energy into empty space to maybe kick out real particles.

These particles go around thousands of times every second. In short, via this process, the Higgs particle was discovered. Which in turn means, there's an invisible field everywhere in the universe; we live in a cosmic superconductor. This means everything we see is an illusion. The properties of the universe that seem like they are designed for us, that make planets, galaxies, stars, the particles that we are made of, etc, are all just an accident. In short, if it wasn't for the Higgs field nothing would be here, nothing would exist, everything would disappear. Our existence is a cosmic accident. Everything is an illusion, including the illusion of design. People think the universe was designed for us because we fit so well into it. Actually we are fine-tuned for the universe, not the other way round. By the way, the Higgs field is close to melting, it could go away. It probably won't, but it could. And even if it does, this will happen in the far, far future. As a result everything we see in the universe will disappear; stars, galaxies, planets, people, absolutely everything will go away."

"Sir," said a female student waving her outstretched hand. "Is it true that we are predominantly made up of neutrons?"

"Yes, we are a bizarre bundle of particles, but predominantly neutrons. The neutron is radioactive.

Neutrons are the most abundant particle in our bodies. The atomic nuclei of atoms have protons and neutrons, but the heavier atoms have more neutrons than protons. The bizarre thing is, if I were to hold a neutron in my hand, it would only 'live' (be stable) for approximately ten minutes before it decays. That's the life span of a neutron. It decays within a short time. So the question now is how come we are here if neutrons have a life time of only ten minutes? Well, it's an interesting accident of nature."

He paused and cleared his throat. "So, the neutron decays into three particles, a neutrino, a proton and an electron. Please note here, the first law of thermodynamics at work, the conservation of energy. You can't destroy energy. It just changes form. Thus, the neutron decays, dies, energy is expelled, and its energy is then converted into those three particles.

Furthermore, the amazing accident is that a neutron and a proton have almost exactly the same mass. The neutron is only slightly heavier. That means the neutron has barely enough mass to allow it to decay because its mass is barely heavier than the sum of the mass of the proton plus the electron plus the neutrino... and because it can barely decay this takes a long time. It takes ten minutes, which does not sound like a long time but in particle physics units that's a very long time. Please note the relativity of time here. Ten minutes in our world, the classical world is a short time. But those ten minutes in the world of particles, subatomic particles, is actually a long time. Thus, this is known as weak decay because it takes so long to happen. But what happens to a neutron when it 'drops' into a nucleus? It becomes bound – that is, it requires energy to come out. So a neutron loses energy here but if we apply E=MC2, the neutron loses energy and therefore loses mass; it loses enough mass so that inside the nucleus it can no longer decay into a proton plus electron plus neutrino. We are only here because of that accident, that the neutron proton mass difference is so small, that when a neutron is in a nucleus it's suddenly stable. And that's the reason why heavy elements, ones that are vital to life, nitrogen, oxygen, iron, carbon can exist... All those nuclei can only exist because this mass difference is so small that when you put the neutrons in a nucleus, they are stable. This is truly remarkable... a remarkable act of existence!! Thus, the mass difference and the force associated with it, are in one sense responsible for our existence, but of course, this is also the force that is responsible for our existence in another sense and maybe the end of our existence! It's the force that is responsible for the nuclear reactions that power the sun; the nuclear reactions that turn hydrogen into helium and produce all the energy that allows life to exist on earth..."

"Professor," said a tame, dry, male voice. It was an android, the one and only in the group. It stood up boldly. It had been constructed six months ago and had been integrated into the group of students... humans. It was on a trial basis in order to see how it would adjust around humans in an academic environment, despite its programming and highly complex mathematical mechanical mind. The android appeared to be something more than human, its black hair, green eyes and pale skin failing to hide its otherness. It said, "Professor you are making a drastic mistake in your reasoning. How is it that you can stand there with such intelligence and yet fail at such a simple level? You're atheistic philosophy makes no sense. Science requires a mind, a force, a mechanism to guide it accordingly. With your highly convoluted explanation of the neutron, it seems you simply regard it as an accident of nature. But to me it's more like a complex arrangement that has been orchestrated via a higher being. Furthermore, you talk about this Higgs field, the Higgs particle. You say that this invisible field is responsible for our existence, and in fact responsible for everything in the universe. The question that I pose to you is this: who put it there? Who designed this particle? How did it get there? The fact that this field has been detected doesn't disprove God's existence. In fact, to my mechanical mind, it suggests that God does indeed exist. He is the eternal Mind that governs the behaviour of particles which He Himself created in the first place. Take the Big Bang. Before this event there was apparently nothing, just a singularity, no space, no time, no matter, nothing, no pre-existent material at all. So the universe literally began from nothing. But that's impossible. It would have had to begin from something, thus it required a cause... God. He caused it and fine-tuned the universe. And it is a fine-tuned universe, science will back that fully... Furthermore, I have been reading books on the theory of evolution, including Charles Darwin of whom I'm sure you are well aware of and I have discovered that many atheists use this theory in order to refute God's ultimate existence. But to me, if evolution is true, God must exist. To me, evolution requires God. Evolution without God makes no sense. Evolution requires a mechanism, a force, a Mind to guide it accordingly. Only an incredibly intelligent, all powerful Mind can control this incredible process. Things cannot self-evolve. I've spoken to many atheists since my construction and entry into your world, the world of humans. Many have fallen into the trap of circular reasoning, the fundamental fallacy in logic. Many have said I disagree with your mechanical conclusion; God does not exist! But all have failed to show a flaw in my arguments and this has led me to the conclusion that God does exist. If you cannot dismantle my argument, nor show a crack in my logic, highlighting where I have gone wrong, you in turn cannot then refute my conclusion that God exists. Thus, their arguments have been nothing but circular...!"

A bitter silence fell... The atmosphere in the room was tense.

"And what of morality Professor...? Excuse the abrupt transition... Without God how does man know what is right and wrong? Science itself is ethically neutral. It does not have a method for determining right and wrong, good and evil. Science tells us how the world works, but it does not tell us how it ought to be. Without God as a transcendent foundation for moral value, man simply becomes lost in socio-cultural relativism. Morality ultimately becomes relative within different environments. This can be dangerous! God has to be the moral guide for mankind, otherwise chaos emerges. Without God, man loses purpose, meaning and morality becomes dangerously subjective."

Seconds of silence fell... All eyes were focused on the android.

"I'll close with this Professor," said the android with electric zest, its eyes ablaze with irrefutable energy. "I'm a biomechanical being, flesh and machine neatly fused together. A machine clothed with skin. I look as human as any of you in the room, but ultimately I'm a machine, a robot. Probability is a massive component of higher-level machine reasoning, using unprecedented processing power to give the most likely answer from a virtually limitless range of knowledge. Androids like me have proven to be astonishingly intelligent and extremely logical. We can solve the most complex of equations and so forth. So if I have come to the conclusion that God must exist, then you need to seriously consider it. I just cannot understand how you Professor, a man of great intelligence, and mankind as a whole, can continue to embrace atheism, pantheism which are one and the same? Again, take me.... I was built as a result of man's desire to achieve and accomplish amazing feats. I am one of the greatest examples of what science can do. I represent engineering at the highest level, physics and mathematics. So the question is: Who gave Man this intelligence to build a machine of my calibre, and many others? From where could man's intelligence stem from? This lies in the realms of epistemology. My answer: It could only have come from the divine. Building a machine of my calibre requires a mind, intellect, calculations and thought process, so surely the atheistic world today, like you Professor, will have to humbly accept that humans too have a maker, a creator...God! My presence here alone should make people think differently. I and many others could be the catalyst in transforming many lives here on Earth. My journey here will be far more significant and important than you think..."

9 O'CLOCK IN THE EVENING

HE moved in frantic haste, like a lost soul getting back to grips with the complex tangle and chaotic confusion of the world. His face dripped with sweat. People were everywhere. New York City was a beehive of activity. As he moved at pace through the crowds, everything passed him in a blur. His heart raced. Within a short time, he reached a section of the city that was almost devoid of people and sound. He gazed up, staring into the heavens in seek of refuge. The moon shone bright and stars flickered in the cold night.

Suddenly, he heard sound. He turned sharply and saw a small nocturnal rodent, hyper-alert, in search of food. Then, looking across to the wall, he saw the familiar poster: A picture of the Android Police. Then the words in black beneath: '*No Escape from the Time Report.*' It cut through him like a knife. Thoughts of the A-Police and how they would use special shields during arrest missions began to race through Hal's mind. The shields were paper-thin, made from a special light-bending material which made the Android police appear invisible. It would work in any environment, day or night.

This light-bending meta-material could make objects, vehicles, buildings, spacecraft and people in general appear invisible. But this technology was reserved for police and military use only. Not only did this special meta-material hide a target in the visible spectrum, but it also worked in the Ultraviolet, Infrared and Shortwave Infrared and it blocked the Thermal Spectrum, making it a very special, almost 'magical' shield in spite of the science involved. There was no power source involved.

Hal turned bitterly away from the poster and saw the somewhat familiar alley. Rapidly he made his way down it, his brisk feet connecting with littered debris. It was dark and dirty, walls peppered with graffiti. Flies circled the air. Escaping the alley he came to a road. He halted, exhaled, then moved on and within ten minutes reached his friend's home. He paused for breath then slowly walked towards the front door. He pressed the buzzer forcefully, trying to regain his composure. A green light flashed signalling positive operation. He heard footsteps. The door opened...

"Hal... my goodness, what happened?"

"Roy, please, we need to talk."

He stepped into the house almost forcing his way through and promptly made his way to the living room. He sat shaking with bitter fear. Fixed to the wall was a large clock, archaic...an antique. He contemplated the hour: 23:36pm. Roy followed him in, obviously mystified... He ran a hand through his thick black hair, his silver ring sparkling in the bright light of the room.

"Drink, double whisky...? You look like you need it," he said invitingly.

"Roy I failed..."

A cold silence fell... Roy sank into a chair, biting his lip.

"Not the Time Report?"

"Yes," Hal replied sharply.

Roy's eyes grew wide with horror. "But why...?"

"You know how they operate... It's a one-off meeting. If you fail that's it."

Roy was suddenly overwhelmed with fear. He understood the implications as did all Earth-citizens. He was almost forty. In a month's time it would be his turn. Hal could see the concern and fear in his friend's eyes.

"Yes Roy. In a month's time it will be your turn. They've already retired Hector. I'm next. Hopefully you won't be."

"Hector," Roy blasted with confused anger, "had many criminal convictions. One could see it coming but you, Hal Johnson, a man of the highest integrity, a professional... a top architect. That's worrying."

"Roy, the government has a bizarre way of making their decisions. There is no prior build up on their part. You enter on the day, they type your name into a computer and your entire life's history is displayed. Once the data is analysed, they decide on the spot whether you are deemed fit to live out the rest of your life and die naturally. It's done within twenty minutes. If they feel you've lived a life below par, then...." he paused, his hands shaking. "I was deemed unfit, thus, retirement. They never gave a justified reason as to why I failed, and that's the same for everyone. They never give a reason. It's either pass or fail. But then again what can you expect from a government that is run by machines. All their laws and decisions are so very mechanical. They may look human, but underneath that skin are a vast array of wires, miniaturised components, intricate circuit boards and powerful motors. They may look human on the outside, but they are nothing but machines, programmed by man. The irony is that they now control the world, the planet. And now there's the Time Report. As far as I'm concerned, their primary objective is to wipe out mankind and they are slowly doing that via the T-Report. Their kind, the androids, will go on, especially now that they have developed the ability to build and construct their own kind in those secret government laboratories; biomechanical robots building biomechanical robots and the process goes on.... I've now got exactly twenty-four hours to prepare. Twenty-four hours from when the decision was made. It's protocol. I failed the T-report at 9pm today. That means I've got twenty-four hours from then to visit family and friends and let them all know the dreadful news. Not much time at all... I'll be picked up at my house tomorrow night at 9pm by those robotic criminals and taken to one of their execution chambers where my life will be terminated via lethal injection..."

He lowered his head and clenched his fists, his knuckles white. He began thinking about his life, friends, family, all the precious moments. He then pictured his execution. What will it be like, he thought, in those final minutes? Hal shook his head and stood up abruptly and looked at Roy, eyes wide and determined.

"No, they won't," he blasted. "No they won't!"

"What," snapped Roy? "What are you saying...?"

"Time to fight back..."

"Fight...? But there's nowhere to hide. It's a lost battle. You can't fight the system. They will hunt you down! Don't forget, we've all been fixed with that damn tracking device. You can run, but they will track you down within no time."

Hal didn't reply. The tracking device would have to be removed as soon as possible he thought. He knew the man that could help...

"Roy, I know I'm a dead man regardless but I'm going to fight these machines the best I can. I'm not going to make it easy for them. The first thing I must do is have the tracking device removed from the back of my neck."

"But how...? Who's going to operate on you? Besides it's a dangerous procedure. You could die."

"I'm already dead Roy. It's time to take risks."

"Fine, but who's going to remove the tracking device?"

"I have a friend, a retired Doctor... a top neurosurgeon. His name is Klaus Reuter. He opposes the government with a passion. He's a sixty year old man from Germany, Berlin. He moved to New York twenty years ago. Once he passed the Time Report in Germany, he decided to move to

America. He has an underground chamber where he still does the odd operation and gets paid well for it. It's illegal of course and deadly secret... Mainly rich people go."

"I don't get it..."

"Basically, many mainstream doctors and hospitals are forced to reject certain individuals. The doctors tell them that their illness is incurable and that there's no hope. Of course, it's not true. These poor human doctors are forced by the government to lie and push innocent civilians away. Those robot... android politicians are behind this. They want to depopulate the world, letting as many human beings die as possible. Not to mention that the world has become over populated, and the medical world can't handle all the demands from the public, so the government has decided to let certain people suffer and wither away. Well, some of these desperate, sick people look for help elsewhere. Many are aware that they are being lied to. I think you get my point. Anyway it's time for me to leave old friend. You probably won't see me again."

Roy stood up with a sparkle in his eyes, a sparkle that his eyes had initially lacked. The expression on his face had completely changed. Hal noticed the sudden transition.

"Wait," he said sharply. "I'm going to help you Hal. Let's see this through together."

"Hold on a second... Do you realise what you are saying Roy?" He paused and gazed into his friend's eyes. "You still have life, hope. Yes, there is no guarantee that you'll pass the Time Report, but you can't just throw your life away for me."

Seconds ticked away. The atmosphere in the room became hard.

"Hal, there is strength in numbers. Please, let me at least try and help you. If I die for the cause so be it! Besides, I've not got much hope when it comes to my meeting with those wretched government android officials in a month's time. Especially after what you have just told me... especially after you informed me that you have failed the Time Report... It's terrifying."

"Roy, I don't know what to say. This is ultimate confirmation of friendship and beyond. If you really feel compelled to help me through this feverish nightmare, so be it, as long as you fully know the implications?"

Roy gave a curt nod, his own certainty reflected in his eyes.

Hal suddenly reached over and hugged him; a hug that transmitted an element of strength and hope. They both knew the odds of survival were very low... Extremely low!

"Okay Roy, let's get out of here. No time to lose. Remember, tomorrow night at 9pm they are expecting to pick me up at my house in order to take me to the execution chamber. Of course I won't be there!" He grimaced. "They will then sound the alarm and start to track me down. With this tracking device in my neck it will be an easy process for them. That's why I need it removed as soon as possible. Now, regarding you, my friend... I know that they are not looking for you, but given that you are now helping me, it would be best for you to have yours removed as well. They may even come here looking for me. They have a list of all my friends, all the information you could possibly think of. If they do come here and find an empty house, they might put two and two together. I think you get my point?"

"Yes, of course..."

"Any objections then...?"

"No Hal, I'll have it removed."

"Great..." he replied with a bounce in his voice. "Yes, I know it's a risky operation but it's a must! It's the first thing we need to do Roy. In terms of payment, we don't need to worry about that. He owes me big time. I've helped him out many times throughout the years. We are very close."

"How long have you known him Hal...?"

"Ten years now..."

"How come you never mentioned him to me in all those years?"

"Doctor Klaus Reuter is a very strange man. There was never a reason to mention him to you, as odd as that may seem."

Outside it started to rain and thunder. The sound was overwhelming. It added to the fearful atmosphere.

They drove in silence. They had left the city of New York and entered the suburbs. The storm had faded. It was pitch black outside... eerily quiet. Across the dashboard, certain readings flashed into life. It glowed with a light greenish haze.

"Okay, that's the building, that's where he lives," said Hal tiredly.

Roy increased velocity for a few seconds then slowed the car down as they approached the small building. The car came to an abrupt halt. Roy checked his watch.

"It is 1am in the morning you know. I hope he's up…"

"This guy doesn't sleep much. He's half-crazed, but then again most brilliant minds are. Besides, he lives in constant fear. He runs an illegal operation, remember. Makes good money, but the fear of being caught torments him."

They stepped out and walked over to the small building, their heels splashing in the dirty puddles of rain. Before they reached the thick steel door, it opened. Klaus emerged dressed in a white lab coat, a tall thin man with cold blue eyes crowning a long pointed nose. He brushed his wild grey hair away from his heavily emaciated face as he peered out at his unexpected visitors.

"Greetings Hal…" Klaus said with a strong Germanic accent. He gazed at his watch, and then looked up somewhat surprised. He then shot a glance at Roy.

He was slightly concerned. Hal could read him like a book.

"It's okay, he's a good friend. I've told him all about you."

Klaus's expression changed. He waved them in without uttering a word. Once they entered he shut the door...

"So what brings you here Hal at this hour?"

"We need to talk... It's so very important."

"I understand. Come let's go to my underground work chamber...We can talk there."

The Doctor ushered them to the seating area in a large brightly lit underground chamber. Three large hygiene beds lay in one corner. Each bed was covered with white sheets. Medical equipment lay scattered throughout, countless bottles filled with strange coloured liquids too. It looked unorganized but clean. There were also several monitors and unusual looking machines. Hal licked his lips as he gathered his thoughts... He said with a calm soft voice, "Klaus, we really need your help..."

"What can I do for you Hal?"

"Remove these tracking devices from our necks."

Klaus stood up and rubbed his jaw. He replied, "Hal, you do realise that I've never attempted such an operation before. Besides, there could be complications. It's a dangerous task... even possible death. Not to mention, it's highly illegal to tamper with those devices. If discovered, the consequences are severe...! Yes, I run an illegal operation here, I've operated on many, cured many, but this is high risk."

"Yes, we are aware..."

"But why Hal...?"

"I've no choice..."

Klaus's eyes grew wide... "I guess that..."

Hal interjected, "Yes... I failed the Time Report Klaus, yesterday at 9pm. They will come for me later today, 9pm exactly. They will pick me up at my house, that's the universal procedure. You know the rest...! As for my friend Roy, he's still yet to go. He's turning forty in a month's time. His appointment is around the corner and he's dreading it. However, he's decided to help me, even at the cost of his own life. He opposes the system... the Time Report... Anyway, in short, we are going to fight to the end.

That's why I need these bugs removed from our necks!"

He pulled back his collar, turned his head, exposing the back of his pale neck in order to emphasize the point.

"I understand," said Klaus with his broken English accent. That strong Germanic tone lingered…"But once removed, we will need to take the tracking devices away. Best thing, throw them into the Atlantic!"

"Yes," replied Hal.

"Tell me, what is your long term plan once the devices are safely removed? It's not easy to fight the system, these damn Androids."

"Plan…? I guess our only option is to leave Terra… head for Mars, or Luna, perhaps even Titan. At least we can buy some time if we leave the planet."

"You and your friend won't make it through customs Hal…"

"That's right," snapped Roy. "It's an impossible mission. We will be arrested at the spaceport."

Klaus' expression changed as if he were about to reveal the penultimate truth. He said, "There is another way to leave Earth and venture out to other planets within our solar-system. It's not a conventional way though..."

"Explain...?" asked Hal eagerly.

"A good friend of mine named Nikolay Dasayev is an American-Russian quantum physicist. He's anti-government, anti-Time Report. He was born in Moscow but moved to the States with his family when he was five." He rubbed his jaw thoughtfully then continued. "Basically, he and his friend, a Professor Victor Polson, a work colleague who is also a physicist, built a very special machine in a secret underground laboratory. And there it remains..."

Hal's eyes grew wide. "What machine?"

"A Quantum Teleportation machine...."

Both Hal and Roy looked at each other....

"Of course it has never been tested... however Nikolay is convinced that it works."

Hal's lips twisted in thought. He said with apprehension, "You say it has never been tested before?"

"Correct. However, as I said, Nikolay is totally convinced that it will work perfectly.... In short, there are basically three kinds of teleportation: The kind where the thing you want to teleport is somehow instantly moved from one location to the other... for example, teleportation through a wormhole. The other kind where your molecules are disassembled, beamed somewhere else, and reassembled in the same way. There are philosophical concerns with this type of teleportation, of course. In particular, the concern when a transporter dismantles the atoms in your body and reassembles in identical arrangement of atoms somewhere else, perhaps the disassembled you actually dies and the reassembled you is actually a new being that just thinks it's you... The last kind is where you scan the object in one place and just transmit the instructions for how to reassemble it somewhere else using different molecules and atoms... In other words, your body is scanned and the information is transmitted somewhere else and used to build an entirely new body out of different materials. This process, the scan-and-reassemble type of teleportation is actually possible thanks to a property of quantum mechanics called, quantum entanglement. Quantum entanglement occurs when two or more particles are forced to hold mutually exclusive states, so determining one simultaneously determines the other. If you have two entangled particles, knowing the state of one will automatically tell you the state of the other as well. So, to summarize, if we take two particles, entangle them, and send one to the moon for example, then we can use that property of entanglement to teleport something between them. If we have an object we want to teleport, all we have to do is include that object in the entanglement. Nikolay uses this method - Quantum Teleportation."

"I guess Roy and I will be the guinea-pigs... this is complex to say the least! It's somewhat risky, no?"

"Yes, I'll be honest, there is an element of risk, of course, but what choice do you have? You need to leave Earth as soon as possible..."

Hal hesitated. His forehead started to run with hot sweat as he contemplated the journey.

"Listen," snapped Roy with zest. "This is a great opportunity to escape the authorities for a time Hal. Think about it, we have no choice in the matter. Let's choose a planet, a moon... Once there we will see what happens..."

"Yes," said Hal... "I agree completely." He turned and looked at Klaus. "Okay, now it's time to remove these tracking devices?"

Klaus smiled and said, "Indeed, but I'm going to need a little rest first. Then time to get things in order. It's no easy operation. Removing these tracking devices is a very delicate, complex process. It won't be easy. Hopefully all will be well."

"I understand," replied Hal.

"Good. Once the anaesthetic is administrated, you'll both fall asleep quite quickly. Not to mention that you'll be out for a lengthy period of time. Upon waking and regaining some composure, we will then head to Nikolay's home. Once all has been relayed to him in terms of your situation, he will then take us to his secret lab, to the Q-T machine. I've been there countless times. I've seen the machine in all its glory..."

Time passed in a flash! Both operations had been successful. Klaus had worked through the early hours of the morning into the early afternoon; 5am until 1.00pm battling the complications that came with the removal of both tracking devices. Both T-devices lay on the concrete floor seemingly inert. They were tiny and metallic, with two short black wires protruding from the centre point of the device itself. As for Hal and Roy, they lay asleep on the hygiene beds dressed in white robes, recovering from the effects of the strong anaesthetic... No bandages were needed.

Suddenly a sound! Hal awoke! He rubbed his eyes, and slowly raised his head and said..."Did you remove them?"

Klaus moved over to him, his feet shuffling with haste against the hard concrete floor...

"Yes, all went according to plan."

He pointed towards the floor. Hal looked down at the two tiny metallic devices with disdain, his eyes somewhat blurred. He then gazed at the hanging, dirt-stained clock and read the time: 4:30pm.

"We should make a move soon Klaus," his voice now regaining some bounce. "Remember the authorities will come for me at my house at exactly 9pm, exactly twenty-four hours after failing the Time report. They will then sound the alarm. Then..."

"Yes, I know. In light of that, get dressed as soon as possible, freshen up and prepare yourself for the ride to Nikolay's. It will take us around forty minutes to get there, plus time to dump those blasted bugs. I'll guide the way."

Hal quickly got to his feet and stretched. In turn, Roy awoke...With semi-closed eyes he turned his head and gazed over...

"I guess all went well?" he said groggily.

"Indeed, both operations were a success. It took some time to remove those damn bugs, but I did it."

Roy moved off the bed and stood up. He saw the two tracking devices lying on the ground.

"I guess that's them?"

"Yes," replied Klaus.

"Look," said Hal sharply, "enough about these bugs. They've been a part of us for too long... Roy, are you going to be okay to drive soon. Say in around half an hour or so?"

"Yes..."

"Great, let's get ready now. We can dump those damn bugs once we are on our way. Time is of the essence." He pointed at the hanging clock. Roy and Klaus followed with their eyes...

They were at Nikolay's house all seated in the front room. It was 6.18pm. The tracking devices had been thrown into the Atlantic prior to their arrival.

"Nikolay," said Klaus. "My friends need your help. It's very serious..."

Nikolay sat there quietly, listening. His large brown eyes shone with energy. He rubbed his head of grey hair and said, "Problems with the government... Do they need an escape...?"

"Yes, correct my dear friend...."

Hal stood up and interjected, "Nikolay to cut a long story short, I failed the Time Report yesterday at exactly 9pm...You know what that means; they will come to my house at exactly 9pm tonight to take me to the execution chamber. I don't have long..." He paused. His eyes grew wide... "As for my friend Roy, he hasn't failed that damn T-report yet, but he's due soon, that is, he's turning forty in a month's time. His appointment is around the corner but he does not trust the system. He has decided to join me in this revolt against the government, even if it means his own life."

"So you and your friend want Quantum Teleportation...correct?"

"Yes," said Hal sitting back down."

"Okay, no problem gentlemen. I can provide the escape from earth as I'm sure you have already been informed by Klaus. However, you must understand that this machine has never been tested but, regardless of this fact, I'm certain all will be well..."

"I've already told them this," said Klaus. "In fact, I went on to explain the quantum science behind it..."

"That's good, that's very good... but before we go further I would like to give you my own explanation regarding Q-T! Quantum teleportation, as it happens, is the only real teleportation technology. You can take some particles in a particular arrangement and transfer their exact quantum condition onto other particles far away. In short you send enough information and energy over to the new location to create the exact arrangement, or state of particles, that corresponds to you. Quantum teleportation has one pivotal property: it is impossible to create an identical copy of a quantum state without destroying the original. In fact you have to destroy the original arrangement in order to extract all the necessary information from it to construct the new teleported state... Please bear this in mind." He rubbed his jaw, his hand grinding into the sharp grey stubble. "Furthermore, teleportation of a quantum state uses the phenomenon of quantum entanglement as a means of transmission. Quantum entanglement is a physical phenomenon that occurs when pairs or groups of particles are generated, interact, or share spatial proximity in ways such that the quantum state of each particle cannot be described independently of the state of the others, even when the particles are separated by a large distance."

"Truly mind-blowing stuff Professor," Roy said, gripped in awe.

"Yes it is, and via this machine, the Quantum Teleportation machine, both you and your friend Hal can exit this planet without detection..." He smiled at the scientific elegance that made all this possible. There was a brief pause and then his eyes lit up... "Furthermore, I have many friends scattered all over the solar-system, Mars, Ganymede, Lunar, Titan... They are all Quantum physicists like me. Once you have chosen a destination, I will contact my friends accordingly to make all the necessary arrangements. They will help you as much as they can once you get to your destination."

"Thank you Nikolay," Hal said. "I owe you big time."

"You owe me nothing. It's a pleasure... Tell me, do you have any questions regarding the machine...?"

"Yes, I do in fact, just one," said Hal. "Is Quantum Teleportation faster than light?"

"There is no faster than light communication or indeed motion in quantum mechanics. Teleportation does not feature any faster than light information transfer..."

"I see..."

"Right, time is short but I have one other piece of information which may give you hope and sustain you through your coming trials," Nikolay said pulling out a small metallic tube from his long brown coat. He lifted his hand high as if he held the key to the elixir of life. The tube sparkled in the light. "My friends, this is the answer to our problem...but it will take time, quite some time, to come to fruition."

"What is that," asked Hal, his eyes fixed on it.

"Once this tube is broken a lethal biomechanical virus will be unleashed, a virus that will eventually wipe out every single android."

"What? Are you serious? That one little thing there...?" Hal snapped.

"Yes Hal. This one little tube has enough power to wipe out every android on Earth, believe me. Don't let its size fool you. Small tube yes, but it's a working atom-bomb which I developed in secret along with my friend and colleague Professor Victor Polson. He too was involved in the construction of the Quantum Teleportation machine along with me... Joint brilliance!"

Silence fell...Everyone was now staring at the metallic tube, agog at its historic significance, contemplating its meaning. Nikolay continued...

"Furthermore, once an android contracts the virus, it is easily and quickly passed on, and within two to three days, the android will shut down, dead if you can even call it that! It's the best and probably only way to exterminate them... And the good thing is the virus can't be stopped! It mutates...thus, once this human-friendly virus is released into the atmosphere, it will kill them off one by one and there is nothing they can do about it..."

"This is truly fantastic," exclaimed Klaus. "But are you sure it's human-friendly?"

"Yes, of course I am. It will have no effect on us at all...Just think of it like a computer virus."

"How long have you had it... the final tube containing virus I mean?"

"Everything was completed and finalised this morning Klaus, at the lab. I then brought it back here with the intention of heading into New York later tonight along with Victor... In short, my plan was, enter the city, break the tube...start the deadly process."

"But why didn't you tell me anything about this earlier Nikolay?

"Klaus I wanted to have it ready in hand before I told you, ready for it to be unleashed as I do now."

"So," said Hal sharply..."Not only have you built this incredible Quantum Teleportation machine, you have also developed a virus that will destroy these damn androids and save humanity."

"Yes correct, I'm a quantum physicist, but my interests stretch into many domains of science including virology. Once you reach a certain level, all the sciences interconnect at the summit, thus it is easy to then develop new skills in other areas."

"So how long will it take to rid the world of these damn freaks," asked Roy staring at the small metallic tube almost transfixed?

"I can't give you an exact date... it will take time, but the victory will be ours!"

"Okay that's it then," said Hal, his voice filled with zest and drive. "That's it... all we need do Roy is to stay away from the planet until the virus has wiped them all out putting an end to the Time report! Once our planet is totally human controlled again we can return safely." He brushed his hand through his hair with relief and then said, "Nikolay, Klaus tells me that this Quantum Teleportation machine is in a secret underground laboratory, correct?"

"That's right. That's where it was built, and that's where it remains."

"How far is this lab?"

"It's about an hour's drive, no more. You can all jump in with me. I've got a big jeep in the garage."

"Okay, well let's leave now. Roy and I need to depart from this planet as soon as possible. Mars, Titan, anywhere will do."

"Fine.... Once we arrive at the lab, you can decide on the exact destination of your choice. I'll do the rest...make all the necessary arrangements with my friends. I'll explain more once we are there."

"Great," said Hal. "On the way, we can drive through New York and unleash the virus as you had originally planned...It's best to do it as soon as possible!"

"Yes, agreed... On the way, I'll call Victor, and tell him the job has already been done!"

A sudden roar cut off his words...

"What was that?" asked Klaus. His eyes widened.

They all stood up and looked towards the window. A police patrol hover-car was parked to the side of the road. Green lights flickered in the early evening twilight. It was starting to get dark.

"It's the android-cops...." blasted Hal in utter shock. His face drained of colour and his eyes popped. "We've got to get out of here... now."

Two androids rushed towards the front door holding beam-rifles, dressed in their standard jet-black uniform. They were so human-like it was eerie. With a series of blasts the door was consumed. All that remained was a cloud of hovering grey dust.

"Hal Johnson…" the androids yelled rushing in, the hard wooden floors creaking. They clutched their long thin beam-rifles tightly, pointing, looking.

In the front room Nikolay, with a trembling hand attempted to break the tube containing the virus, but instead, dropped it. It hit the floor intact, cushioned by the grey carpet beneath. Instantly Hal knelt, picked up the tube, and momentarily attempted the same, but failed. The androids rushed into the front room.

Hands shaking, he managed to fumble it into his left trouser pocket. He stood back up with heightened colour in his cheeks. One of the androids then marched over to him at a mechanical pace saying, "No one escapes a failed Time Report." Reaching him, the android halted, raised its beam-rifle and swung it towards Hal's face. The rifle connected sharply with his jaw. The impact was hard. Hal instantly fell to the ground... Blackness swirled around him, then.....

Hal awoke. He was lying on a hygiene bed in a small dimly lit room, virtually unable to move, as if he had been paralyzed by a strong narcotic.

"Please relax," ordered the cold semi-humanoid voice. "It won't take long. The neurotoxic venom has already been administrated via injection. As for your three heroic friends, they have all been retired for their crimes respectively."

Hal's sickly face was overwhelmed with sadness.

"Don't worry... you'll soon be joining them."

Hal grimaced. He was consumed with both hate and fear. He turned his head with pain and realised that he was in an execution chamber. His good friends Roy and Klaus were now dead; so too the mysterious Professor Nikolay Dasayev, the great Quantum Physicist and inventor. He was next. He saw the android standing tall. It looked more human than human, blond hair, green eyes, skin, flesh, even the bodily aroma of human! But it wasn't!

"How did you know I was on the run?" asked Hal groggily. "I mean it wasn't anywhere near the pickup time of 9 o'clock?"

"Mr Hal Johnson, from the very moment that the tracking devices were tampered with and eventually removed, we here at the government were alerted. From that moment, we zeroed in. We scanned the location of the T-devices then listened in via the T-devices. From there, we monitored all discussion... including the discussion you had in the car on the way to Professor Nikolay Dasayev's home. Once the T-devices were thrown into the sea, we simply listened in via the car's monitoring system. Remember all cars are bugged too...There's no escape."

Hal was overwhelmed by a deathly cold... but then he suddenly recalled the tube containing the virus. The one he had slipped into his left pocket. It hit him all at once! He moved his hand slightly and felt the small deadly bulge. It was still intact waiting to be broken... He was filled with sudden importance... '*Break the metallic tube and I win regardless*,' he thought... '*saving countless souls throughout the course of time.*' He viewed his imminent death as if he were a martyr saving all humanity. He smiled, his eyes distant and reflective. He said... "You have taken away the soul of Man for a time, but your reign will soon come to an end!"

He wriggled his fingers and joy surged through him as he found he had enough movement to slip his left hand slyly into his pocket where the tube containing the lethal biomechanical virus nestled. With a finger and thumb he squeezed hard and this time managed to break it before the creeping cold and numbness engulfed his fingers. He was elated, overwhelmed that he had fulfilled the task, but this was tempered by the realisation that he wouldn't live to see the result. The virus would now spread wildly, wiping out all organic-robots... The victory was his... humanity's! He smiled and spoke for the last time, "This world belongs to us...there can be only one ruler and we are soon to reclaim it." With that, Hal Johnson breathed his last at exactly 9 o'clock in the evening....

LAST ROBOT

THE last robot had been built for the last time. Newly formed legislation implemented by world government was as follows: Construction of robots - forbidden! AI was now prohibited! Governments throughout the planet had clamped down hard. Terra (Earth) was infested with machines. Stats indicated that for every human there were four robots. This became a major concern...

"It claims to have dreamed, dreamed, would you believe," rasped Marshall Zielinski, the lines on his forehead deepening.

Sebastian Nowak shrugged as his feeling of wonder grew more acute. "I just don't get it Marshall." He paused and rubbed his thick beard that was slowly being invaded by grey... "Its brain shouldn't operate any differently from the others. Strange that the last robot built claims to have dreamed and on multiple occasions I believe... years of study, decades of analysing robotic brain patterns, now this. I'd love to see how its patterns have altered."

"Yes, bizarre," exclaimed Marshall.

"Tell me, when is it due to receive clearance?"

Marshall replied with a steady voice, "It will be released into the outside world in two days time. We are just waiting for the government to send us the A-Card, that's why the delay. After that it will be granted clearance and will enter the streets of our beautiful New York." He paused in reflection then continued. "Well at least it's given the engineers more time with it. As a result, look what we have discovered!"

"Indeed! But it's so sad that AI Special Technologies will be shut down all over the world because of the new government law. They fear a robotic takeover. Stats suggest that for every human there are four robots. We are outnumbered. Still, it's a big mistake, and soon we will all be out of a job, but regardless, our names will be etched in history throughout the ages to come."

"Yes Sebastian. Our names shall be remembered..."

There was a light knock.... The door opened and a head popped in.

"It's ready, and it's here," said one of the head technicians, Dale Thomson. He smiled so that wrinkles creased about the corners of his mouth.

Permission for it to enter was quickly granted by both men with a mute nod. Dale immediately pushed the door open further. The tall metallic robot now came into view. It stepped into the room and said, "Greetings my creators."

Dale left their presence and shut the door tight.

"Take a seat," invited Sebastian.

It moved towards a large chair and sat crossing its legs. Seconds of silence passed...

"So, tell me X-11, tell me how you know that you have dreamed?" enquired Sebastian.

"Well," it said. "It goes like this... Previously, whenever I reached a point where fatigue set in, I closed my eyes in order to recuperate. Each time there was total darkness until I reopened them and once again connected with the reality of the world. But suddenly things changed." It paused... "I've simply never experienced anything like it. As a result I searched my mind, my vast vocabulary, to try to give meaning to what was happening. I came across the word 'dream'. After close examination of its meaning I came to the clear conclusion that I had been dreaming. Up until then, I thought it might have been a mechanical brain malfunction, some kind of flaw."

"How many times have you dreamed X-11?" asked Marshall curiously.

"Six. And each time it was as if I entered another dimension, another realm...the ultimate reality."

"What do you mean by ultimate reality?" Marshall said.

"My dreams felt more real than this, more real than anything I've experienced here within this reality."

Sebastian looked over at Marshall. Their eyes, old with wisdom, met for a few seconds as the tension in the room grew...

"You do realize why we are so perplexed by this revelation X-11?" said Sebastian. "Only humans dream, some animals too, like cats and dogs, but a robot! This is truly remarkable. Humans dream so that the brain can reorganize itself. The brain is such a complex organ, it needs it. It now appears that you X-11 are undergoing a similar process, as bizarre as that is, only that your brain is mechanical. As far as we know you are the only one, the only robot to ever do so." Sebastian paused and gazed deeply into its eyes... "From a human perspective, dreams in general X-11 are nothing other than vivid sensorimotor hallucinations with a narrative structure. It's all to do with chemical alterations within the brain, brain chemistry, but ultimately it's not real, regardless of how real it might seem. But your case takes this into a completely new sphere altogether, a new sphere of metaphysics... given that you are a robot. Tell me X-11... tell me about your first dream. What did you see?"

The robot appeared to become nervous, almost a mechanical twitch; a microscopic twitch. It remained quiet for a short time as though complex calculations were going through its head. It looked towards the floor then turned its head smoothly towards Sebastian and said...

"I saw a world, a planet, planet Earth infested with machines. "It paused... "Robots were everywhere, in surface-cars, hover-cars, standing on balconies, streaming in and out of buildings, gossiping even. Very few humans were visible, a few standing out between the crowds of metal in the open air marts, where merchandise from the wealthy colonies of Ganymede and Mars was sold."

"What about dream two....?" asked Marshall, his eyes alight with intrigue.

"As for dream two, it was merely a repeat of the first. In fact, dreams one, two, three, four and five were all exactly the same... identical."

"And dream six...?" Sebastian asked rubbing his jaw.

The phone suddenly rang severing the flow of the discussion. Marshall sprang towards it and answered.

"Hello..."

"Is this Marshall Zielinski?"

"Speaking..."

"This is Leslie Weinstein from the government AI control board." The voice that spoke was hard, tense. Ripples of urgency were clearly detectable.

"Is this to do with X-11's A-card?"

"It's to do with X-11 alright and the others."

Crackles of static followed...

"Tell me, where is X-11 right now?"

"It's here with me...We are having a meeting."

"Has it claimed that it has been dreaming?"

Marshall hesitated then replied, "Yes, as a matter of fact it has, six times. Why?"

"I thought so," snapped Leslie. "Has it told you about its dreams?"

"Yes, but only the first five. You interrupted us with this call..."

"Okay, listen carefully Zielinski. Government AI-inspectors throughout the United States, and the rest of the world, Germany, Holland, Russia, China, Japan etc, have all reported that robots are now claiming to be dreaming; over ninety-five percent in total... a staggering figure. That's practically all of them."

Marshall's face went red with surprise. His eyes grew wide. Instinctively he turned towards Sebastian holding onto the phone stunned, knuckles white. "It's Leslie Weinstein from the government AI control board. It's been reported that over ninety-five percent of all robots worldwide are now dreaming."

"What?" snapped Sebastian...

He leapt towards Marshall so that he could listen in. As for X-11, it just sat there motionless like an inert lump of refined metal.

"Zielinski, listen," rasped Leslie. "Do not repeat anything as of now, it might be dangerous..."

Marshall held the phone tightly. He started to sweat a little... Sebastian stood beside him listening in, his heart pounding.

"All the world governments have come to a joint irreversible agreement that as of now, every single robot throughout the planet will be terminated with immediate effect. That obviously includes X-11, the last robot ever built."

A cold bitter silence fell. The atmosphere in the room was hard. Both Marshall and Sebastian were left in shock. Not only was AI Special Technologies going to be closed down globally, the one and only elite agency that had mastered AI and had built every single machine to date, it was now going to lose all its robots. Years of mathematics, equations, robotic engineering and computer science was ultimately going to be binned and forgotten.

Marshall gripped the phone tighter, oblivious to the ray of sunlight that filtered in through the window and warmed his faced. He replied, "But Leslie... why?"

Leslie cleared his throat and said, "We already had our fears here at the AI control board. This fear was felt globally," Leslie rasped. "For every human there are four robots as you know. This is the reason why AI Special Technologies is being closed down for good throughout the world, in order to ensure that no more robots will ever be built. At the rate you guys were going we would have eventually been dangerously, and I repeat, dangerously outnumbered, thus the decision to close you down. But the government's decision to wipe out all currently living robots was made for another reason."

"And the reason is," asked Marshall cynically.

"We have now discovered what all these robots have been dreaming about... The reports are as follows.... Every single robot has claimed to have had six dreams just like X-11. And they have all mysteriously had the same dreams. Identical. This is what is so worrying, so strange."

Marshall looked at Sebastian. Their eyes met like an explosion! Leslie continued...

"In short, they have all said that the first five dreams were exactly the same. X-11 too, I gather?"

"Yes," replied Marshall bitterly. "Correct."

"Furthermore, they all said that in their dreams, the first five, they saw a world, a planet, our planet Earth infested with machines, and that robots were everywhere, in surface-cars, hover-cars, standing on balconies, etc... and that very few humans were visible, a few standing out between the crowds of metal in the open air marts, etc... Is that what X-11 described to you?"

"Yes," replied Marshall.

"Now for the punch-line...! In the final dream, dream six, they all said that they saw a war taking place between man and machine, robots snaking through the ruins and ash, emerging as masters. They then saw a huge crystal-like city gleaming with splendour, swarming with thousands and thousands of jubilant robots. A certain robot then emerged, standing high on a balcony. All the robots bowed saying... *All hail X-11 our leader and god! Mankind is now forever extinct...!*

Behind the two men standing motionless in shock by the telephone, X-11 uncoiled silently and smoothly from the chair. Its cold robotic eyes fixed on its creators as it readied itself to decommission them and fulfil the promise of its dreams...

A BRIEF MOMENT IN TIME

IT sat inside the smooth, triangular-shaped time-machine. Within its shell, there was a mass and tangle of snaking wires and humming steel boxes. All the mathematical calculations had been made by human minds. The android would soon become a pioneer; the first ever to move through the scatter flow of time and taste the bitter stench of a past world. No human had dared, but this biomechanical machine was willing and was about to make history.

Brian, as it had been named, was going to briefly observe the land of Ancient Greece during the time of Plato. There was to be no interaction with the people in any form because of the possible consequences, the possible dangers; chaos theory. After all, its presence alone could alter history, the present, and in turn, the future but observing from afar was considered only a very minor risk, one mankind was willing to take, and so too, the willing android, in spite of the dangers that faced it. After all, there was no guarantee that it would survive the journey even one way and it was a two-way journey. Regardless, this was no deterrent. As far as it was concerned, it didn't really exist anyway. There was nothing to lose.

It checked the intercom then put on its oxygen helmet so that bacteria would not be introduced into the ancient atmosphere. It had to be kept on at all times. It pushed the golden-lever forward. Its fingers twitched. Colourful dial-light shone brightly across the oxygen helmet. It smiled, devoid of any fear. But what was to fear? It was a skin-covered robot after all; a biomechanical machine. Real fear is nothing other than a thalamic impulse experienced only by the refined human mind. As it sat in the silver-metal triangular chamber of roaring light, there was a strange aroma which it detected via sensors in its nostrils. A fusion of many wonderful and wild aromas melted into one.

Its highly complex robotic mind started to consider the following: '*This time-machine might be used as an escape vehicle for many in the future. Some might want to journey back in time with the intention of remaining within that particular past reality in order to escape the petty, corrupt real world of today. But philosophically this has serious implications.*'

It now focused, staring rigidly at the thick glass window ahead. Suddenly, there was an eerie sound, as if all time had ceased. The time-machine started to shake, and vibrate. Its arms trembled. It went dark and all time blazed in this momentary darkness. The time-machine now began to shake and jolt even more as it passed a particular moment in time; the time when Android Brian had been constructed and breathed its first. Then, there was day, then night.... day, night, day, night and then something in between; a strange almost unexplainable twilight. Time was like a film run backward, it suddenly thought!

Then, all at once the machine stopped shaking and vibrating. There was no sound. It looked ahead. All it could see was a thick fog. But the fog that enveloped the machine soon blew away and golden sunlight shone and in the ancient light, the landscape before it began to take shape and form; ancient Greece... It pressed the eject button, releasing the door glittering with sun and looked out into the morning.

It saw birds majestically circling a clean crystal blue sky. It seemed like Brian was looking, studying the very atoms of the air itself. The grass beneath was moist. It was time, but it had to be careful. Under no circumstances was it to interact with the people in anyway only observe from afar, as complicated as that would be! A ripple effect through time would be disastrous. It could potentially mean, no Italian Renaissance, best known for its achievements in painting, sculpture, architecture, literature, philosophy, music, science and technology, and exploration. No Christopher Columbus, thus no discovery of the new world, thus no United States. No Galileo, Machiavelli, Giordano Bruno. No Enrico Fermi, who started the atomic age, and so on. So it had to be extremely careful even when stepping over plants. Yes, something as trivial as that! Even crushing a plant could cause a domino effect, a small ripple that could upset balances and create a catastrophic ripple through time. Brian's dangerous mission was about to begin....

Time, relatively speaking, passed....

The time-machine just suddenly appeared...a sudden mass. It sat in the same room, in the same position as it had prior to departure. Brian removed the oxygen helmet, placing it on the metallic floor. It deactivated the time-machine which ceased operating immediately... total silence. It pressed the eject button, releasing the door, and stepped out, marking the floor with a bit of ancient mud. Sunlight poured down on Brian from the one small, high, window. It noted a tiny difference to the ancient sun it had seen. Brian's eyes held an unusual glow. Its clothes smelt odd, strange; the scent of the past. It breathed in, and the faint scent of chemicals in the air met with its nostrils, barely detectable, but its inner senses declared it was there. Professor Anthony N. Hitchens stood in eager anticipation.

"It worked! Your journey was a success Brian. Tell me, what happened, what did you see?"

Brian stood there silent for moment, and in that pause its body was overcome with emotion. Even though it was an android best suited for such a task, it felt overwhelmed by the experience. It rubbed its smooth jaw, and said, "I saw Ancient Greece in all its glory. I saw the beautiful landscape, the refined buildings, and the people dressed in their wonderful costumes. I stood afar and simply observed without being noticed. I was very careful, extremely so."

"Brilliant," snapped the Professor. "So tell me more."

"What else is there to tell? I achieved the task with caution and have made history."

"Indeed you have Brian..."

The android now walked over to a chair and sat. It crossed its legs and said, "This wonderful experience has made me think deeply, Professor."

"That's good. What are you thinking exactly?" The Professor pulled up another chair and sat rubbing his hands, staring intently at the robot before him.

"Well, regardless of the technological changes and advancements throughout the course of time, and the knowledge that has been progressively acquired, which in turn has revolutionized the world, this time-machine being the prime example, and an android of my complexity, there is a common element that unifies man throughout history." It paused, then, continued. "Mankind is still in search of meaning; the meaning of their existence. I journeyed back to the time of the great philosophers of ancient Greece, the time of Plato. But it seems to me that Mankind is still puzzled about why they exist, why the universe exists, and so forth. And ultimately what propelled life into being?"

The Professor graciously said, "Brian, I'm taken aback by your deep thinking. You have highlighted a very important, vital, fundamental point! The question of why does anything at all exist, is so important to answer. Human beings throughout the ages have indeed been left puzzled by these philosophical questions. Even today many are uncertain, and try to use complex science to find the answer. But the answer to all those questions lies in theology, not science. Science has its limitations.

Science has explained so much with regard to the universe, the physical laws that govern the cosmos and so forth, yet it has been unable to go beyond... Science doesn't give a purpose for this universe coming into being. It gives details of how it came about but it does not explain why. In actuality, science is based on steps of faith... hypothesis, theory. Science is actually transitional. It evolves as human knowledge expands. In fact, the approach of faith is actually scientific in nature. Thus, as I said, the answer to those questions lies in theology, that is, God, the creator of all; He propelled all life into being. As a result, all of reality can be explained by Him. And to enter into a relationship with Him, in spirit, for us humans, is the key to life... Now many scientists have rubbished the existence of God. Some have said, that the divine spark that created life in the first place is not so divine, that is the discovery of complex amino acids in space, biochemistry, tells us that it is quite likely that the complex organic molecules on which life is based either arose in space or developed on earth. Furthermore, they say that through the laws of physics they can show how all matter was created and that through the laws of physics, chemistry and biology we can explain everything without the need for God. Theology ultimately corrupts and inhibits the human soul. We do not need it! But these atheistic scientists are wrong. God exists, and His creation declares it. He holds all matter together. In fact, science and God work together. They are not diametrically opposed as many think. Science has not buried God. In fact science reveals that God must exist. Science and God have important mutual interests. More due diligence and inquiry on the subject will reveal such.

Furthermore, many scientists say that you can create a universe from nothing with galaxies, stars, etc, without the need of supernatural intervention. Now in order to make sense of this, we need to look at the definition of nothing. Nothing is a physical concept because it is the absence of something, and something is a physical concept. The simplest kind of nothing is the kind of nothing in the bible, an infinite empty space, an infinite dark void, thus nothing in it, no particles, no radiation, nothing. Well, that kind of nothing turns out to be full of stuff in a way much more complicated than you would have imagined. Due to the laws of quantum mechanics and relativity, we now know that empty space is a bubbling brew of virtual particles that pop in and out of existence at every moment. Thus, with that kind of nothing, according to atheistic scientists, if you wait long enough, you are guaranteed by the laws of quantum mechanics to produce something from seemingly nothing. They say that when you add gravity into the mix, a natural miracle occurs. That is, gravity allows negative energy as well as positive energy configurations. Thus you can create two particles out of nothing, then eventually matter, then a universe filled with life. In short, in order to create something, you don't need anything. But that's impossible. The laws of quantum mechanics alone cannot create physical realities... life! Thus the laws of quantum mechanics cannot bring anything into existence. Physical laws are a description of what normally happens under certain given conditions. Laws are not responsible for bringing anything into existence regardless of the fact that empty space is not really empty. God uses the laws of quantum mechanics which he himself brought about in order to bring life into existence. In conclusion, he created every invisible particle, thus he controls the laws of quantum mechanics and relativity. Empty space is not empty because he designed it that way. Furthermore, these atheistic scientists have gone one step further and have tried to answer the question of where the space came from. Now, no space could be considered as the ultimate definition of nothing. Again their atheism has led them to this conclusion and I'm now going to quote the very words of a famous atheistic scientist, Peter J. Keegan. He says, '*Now a more demanding definition of nothing is no space, but in fact once you apply the laws of quantum mechanics to gravity itself, then space itself becomes a quantum mechanical variable and fluctuates in and out of existence and you can literally by the laws of quantum mechanics create universes, create spaces, and times, where there was no space and time before. The laws of science, physics, and nature could be considered something, too. Furthermore, there may be an infinite number of universes and in each universe that's been created, the laws of physics, including classical space maybe different; it's completely random and the laws themselves come into existence when the universe comes into existence. So there is no pre-existing fundamental law. Anything that can happen does happen, therefore, you have no laws, no space, no time, no particles, no radiation... and that's the ultimate definition of nothing!*

Now let's review this quote: In short, it makes no sense. The laws of quantum mechanics cannot by themselves create anything, let alone apparent universes, spaces, times, where there was no space and time before. If you go along with this thinking, you are basically ascribing creative power to physical law, i.e., quantum mechanics. But laws don't create anything, let alone a complex universe, space. Only the will of God could have brought space, the universe into existence. If you remove God from the equation, you are ascribing creative power to physical law. In summary the laws of physics, quantum mechanics, can't cause anything to happen... only the will of God could be responsible for the existence of space, the universe, and indeed all matter. Now, in order to prove the existence of this Creator, let's further examine the definition of nothing, and move on from there. There are a variety of forms of nothing, they all have physical definitions. The laws of quantum mechanics tell us that nothing is unstable. 70% of the dominant stuff in the universe is nothing. There's nothing there, but it has energy. Nothing weighs something. Nothing is almost everything. Quantum mechanical systems and the quantum vacuum are physical realities, therefore clearly something. You cannot call these realities, nothing! Thus, all things need an explanation for their existence. Now, there are two kinds of things; things that exist necessarily and things that exist contingently. Let me explain. Things that exist necessarily exist by the necessity of their own nature. Thus it's impossible for them not to exist. Examples, numbers, mathematical objects exist in this way. Now this seems plausibly true. By contrast things that are contingent do not exist necessarily. They exist because something else has caused them to exist, examples being physical objects, planets, man, animals, galaxies. Now, let's look at the universe. The universe is all of physical reality, all matter and energy. So, if the universe has a cause for its existence, that cause must be a non-physical immaterial being that dwells beyond space and time. A number does not fit that description, that is, an abstract object cannot cause anything to happen. For example, the number 5, an abstract object, can have no effect on anything. In fact God is the best explanation for the applicability of mathematics to the physical world. Mathematics is the language of nature. The applicability of mathematics to the physical world proves that a mechanism is at work... God! God designed the universe on the mathematical structure he had in mind. Thus if you accept atheism, in turn you have to say that the applicability of mathematics to the physical world is just a bizarre coincidence... Now, jumping ahead, let's look at the fine-tuning of the universe. In short, a fine-tuned universe requires God. Only God could have done this. In fact, the initial conditions of the big bang were fine-tuned for the existence of the universe and intelligent life, with a precision that's mind blowing. The laws of nature are expressed in mathematical equations and you find appearing in them certain constants like the gravitational constant. The values of these constants are independent of the laws of nature and nature operates under certain laws like entropy. These laws are so delicate and refined that a slight alteration in them would mean no life anywhere in the cosmos. Thus, the life permitting balance within the universe is so finely tuned that only God could be responsible for it. Thus, the fine-tuned universe declares God's existence... But of course, atheists will attack the theistic version of the fine-tuned universe. So, let's examine their objection via an analysis of the only three possible explanations for such a universe. The first is physical necessity, the second, chance and the third one, which I've already mentioned, design, a designer, God. Physical necessity is not however a plausible explanation because the finely-tuned constants and quantities are independent of the laws of nature. Therefore they are not physically necessary. So could the fine-tuning be due to chance? The problem with this explanation is the odds of a life permitting universe governed by the laws of nature are so infinitesimal that they cannot be reasonably faced. It's beyond ridiculous, and totally illogical. Thus, the proponents of chance have been forced to resort to a bizarre metaphysical hypothesis, namely the existence of the multiverse, infinite in number and randomly ordered so that life permitting universes would appear by chance. This hypothesis is fantastically outrageous. My objection; there's no mathematics to back such a bizarre theory. The lack of scientific evidence says it all! So chance is not a plausible explanation, but design is. And it's the best and only explanation. Thus the fine-tuning is the best evidence for a cosmic creator. Therefore, the cause of the universe must be a transcendent mind that exists eternally. This transcendent mind, God, is the uncaused cause to the universe, and any other potential universe, or universes that 'may,' exist. Even if the bizarre multiverse theory were true, it's not eternal. It would still require a creator. God transcends the physical universe, including both space and time. He is the timeless, immaterial, personal creator of everything in the universe including space and time; a non-spatial non-temporal being.

Now, another proof for God's existence lies in moral philosophy. A close examination into the existence of ethics and morality, the anthropological argument, reveals that there must be a God, right and wrong, good and evil. In fact the whole purpose of life is connected to morality and ethics. Thus God is the best explanation for objective moral values. There are certain morals which are objectively binding and true. For example, killing a human being for no reason would fall into this category. This is an immoral act. But in the naturalistic view, there's nothing objectively wrong with this. In other words, naturalists would say, moral values are subjective products of biological evolution and social conditioning. Thus, there is no right or wrong, good or evil, only will, therefore no purpose or meaning to life. In fact, atheism equates to no purpose to life and the universe. That in turn implies that there is no purpose to morality or ethics. This view falls into the category of nihilism... In contrast, a theist grounds objective moral value in God, therefore a believer has the explanation to justify objective moral values and duties. And those objective moral values and duties exist in accordance with that belief. Without God, ethics and morality become subjective. Without God, objective moral values don't exist. Without God being at the centre of our lives, the very foundation of our being, man is lost, without hope, without direction. By replacing God with reason and empirical inquiry, chaos occurs within the realms of moral philosophy."

Seconds of deep silence passed... The android Brian stood up, its eyes ablaze with energy. It said, "Your deep explanation into the meaning of life via science, philosophy and of course ultimately theology is breathtaking Professor. I'm totally overwhelmed. There is no doubt in my mind that this God that you talk of exists. But the one question, I put to you is this, can a man-made machine, an android, a robot like me ever connect with this God?"

D4 DETECTIVE

TONY Fletcher lay in the dark, wrapped up in an electric-blanket, in near-lightless obscurity. Outside, sporadic bursts of lightning lit the cold night sky an intense white. Rain came down hard. *'Another blasted day hunting down that one crazed android D4,'* he thought bitterly. *'Just wait till I get my hands on you!'* His eyes flickered; his lips twitched. He felt a minor constriction in his chest, but that soon passed. In the corner of the room the T-Set played at an audio level that was just enough to satisfy him. A documentary on AI had started. This was of particular interest to him, given that he, as a detective, was now responsible for tracking down a crazed organic robot and retiring it accordingly. The voice on the screen said:

'Many androids are now expressing a great interest in astrophysics and, astrobiology. Their studies of astronomy and living organisms in space are being used in various universities around the United States to help in the respective fields...' An android appeared on the screen, and its sharp green eyes shone beyond those of any human, and its brown hair was rich. It was being interviewed. It said... *'Light does not always travel at the same blistering speed. Only in a vacuum does it have its maximum velocity.'*

Tony thought of the sun, the swirl of atoms, all moving along their hammering trajectories, hugely complicated. The voice of the commentator returned. It went on to say:

'The development of computer science has produced a new kind of thinking, that is, how do you describe a process? For example mathematics is good at describing things, geometry and mechanics, like the differential equation for a solar-system. With the notion of a computer, it's all about how can I make something that learns while adapting to its environment? How can I make something that stores responses to a billion different situations and changes and adapts? Indeed all this requires great philosophy. How do we describe all these complicated processes that we are made of? When we consider the human brain, no one knows how the nerve cells in the central nervous system work. The human brain is the greatest mystery of all! Many say that the brain is a biological thing, very different from a computer. The shapes of the cells in the human brain are variable and curved whereas the shapes of machines are squared. The brain is very different from the rest of biology, that is, it is a separate machine. In most of biology there are many interactions. But with the brain, each brain cell is more or less separate from the others, that is, it is a separate machine. It's bathed in a bath of chemicals... but those chemicals are very carefully controlled. The cells of the nervous system are

the closest thing in the universe to the transistors and gates of a computer. In short, a biological brain is the closest thing to a computer, regardless of the different processes involved. Most of the brain is cortex....it has a billion or more cells. The human brain is a certain size because it has to be in order to accommodate enough cells to make you human...'

He started to drift off, but fought it, and then heard....

'The goal was to make a machine with the kind of versatility and resourcefulness that we take for granted in humans. The way in which that was achieved was to package a lot of different ways to represent knowledge and a lot of different ways to exploit it into that machine. This led to a particular question, that is, is there a central place in a mechanical brain that is in charge of everything, and thus, knows everything? The answer, no, it can't be. Reason... because different kinds of knowledge are represented in different ways. Many philosophers today ask what does it mean for a machine to be conscious...? Dr Alan Di Vinci argues that, "The phenomenon of consciousness is complicated and overrated. People act as if they know what they are thinking and so forth, but in fact, the truth is... you don't even know where you got your next sentence from, nor do you know where random words are coming from and what makes you think of them..." 'Furthermore,

in terms of AI development, in order for a machine to have a goal, it has to have some kind of picture or representation or description of a future situation.'

Tony battled with the desire to sleep again, but fought it and recaptured the moment....

'Having an active goal is to have a description of a future situation, and the present situation, and then a process which does things to make them the same by changing the present situation.... In terms of humans, what type of goals do we have? Well, evolution provides the vital ones like the urge to eat and drink for survival purposes.'

Tony did fall asleep but then something deep inside him prompted him to reawaken; a sudden reaction within his deeply convoluted biological mind... His eyes opened and he heard....

'There is no such thing as consciousness per say... That is, there is so much complex activity within the brain, a multitude of processes that regulate memory, emotion and so forth that it becomes impossible to explain consciousness. Neuroscience knows how neurons connect to each other via complex synapses, conductors. That is, neurons send chemicals to the next neuron and start complex activities...The human brain is like eight-hundred different computers, hundreds of different structures that each work in different ways.

In contrast, computers are made of transistors which make up a prototype form of consciousness, that is, robots can self reflect. Remember, androids don't have millions of years of evolution and social cognition like humans, and yet in some ways, they exceed man. In narrow categories, machines exceed human brilliance by a distance; a cohesive complex intelligence system...'

A sudden philosophical thought hit Tony hard, invoked by the tele-set... *'What does it mean to be human?'* This thought worked like a catalyst, and opened his mind... *'I'm a person, a seemingly independent entity that breathes and thinks with a brain that is made of cortical columns. I'm body and mind, a symbiotic network. But perhaps this is just an illusion. Perhaps there's something even greater that defines who I am. Perhaps my spirit, my soul, which is a nexus of electromagnetic forces, defines the real me...'*

He was lost in deep thought for a time. But then, he slowly drifted off to sleep...

The next day found Tony in the New York police headquarters, dressed in his familiar long grey coat and black shirt. His deep philosophical thoughts from the previous night were now dismissed. It was business time! He sat in his office awaiting the arrival of his boss, James Grainger. Heaped across the desk, almost in a mathematical arrangement, were various documents and papers. Pinned to the wall was a large detailed picture of D4, the killer android! Cold blue eyes, blond hair, chiselled face. The angel of death!!! Each android had an individual serial number engraved on its forehead. He looked at it with controlled anger and fiddled with the inner topography of his left ear with a forefinger to nullify an itch. Suddenly, the door swung open. James strolled in.

"Morning detective..."

"Morning, Sir!" he replied sharp-eyed.

James was a tall man, middle-aged, with grey hair, clean shaven. His upper cheeks were sun-darkened, his lower face pale. He sat down facing Tony on the opposite side of a desk and rolled up his sleeve, consulting his gold wristwatch.

"Tony, you need to move fast now. Time is of the essence. Track it down and terminate it as quickly as possible!"

"Don't worry Sir, I'm working on it."

"Good. Remember, it's already killed ten people."

"Yes, and all of them male and all of them killed the same way, with a single gunshot to the head!"

James ran his hand along his jaw, as if to confirm by touch that the flesh really belonged to him. He contemplated, and said, "Yep, and as a result the city of New York is now living in terror. That's why you need to find it and retire it as soon as possible Tony before others are killed..."

Seconds of weighted silence passed...

Scratching his forehead, Tony replied, "Yes, of course Sir. Don't worry, I'll get it soon, believe me." He grimaced. "But this is one bizarre case.... I mean androids have to abide by the standard laws of robotics. They are all programmed to do so and follow instructions accordingly. But this one has somehow gone crazy. This shouldn't be happening. Bizarrely it seems to be filled with anger and resentment. This Frankenstein-being should be following the standard laws of robotics like the others, but it doesn't..."

"Well Tony, many think that this is down to some kind of computer virus, or perhaps the robot manufacturers down at Takahashi Robotics made a serious error with this one. Remember, these mechanical brains that they manufacture are extremely complex. The more complex, the higher the probability of an error occurring. The mathematics they use in working out robotic brain-pathways is highly complex and convoluted to say the least."

Tony stood up and looked out of the window anxiously. He focused on the surface-vehicles below in a reflective blur... He then turned and faced his boss.

"You know what's really worrying me? What if some of the other androids carry the same potential defect? I mean, D4 started out alright but now it has turned into a killer. The implications here are vast... Even the press, who have started attacking the robot manufacturers down at Takahashi Robotics about this defective robot, have expressed the same concern. As a result of all these factors, Takahashi Robotics could, in future, be shut down for good. Not to mention that all the androids that have been integrated into society throughout the globe could, in time, be potentially retired, which would mean a world with no more androids. This will have an impact on society, no doubt, but we humans can readapt. We lived without them before. It will take time to readjust, given that these robots occupy many important roles in science now... space-projects like terraforming Ganymede and Titan, engineering, and so forth..."

"Yes, Tony, but many will argue that mankind needs machines regardless of this bizarre situation with D4, and the possible future consequences that it may bring. Mankind simply hasn't got the stamina or faculty to continue managing this complex world alone without the aid of machines. Let's face it, androids have, and are helping us to undertake some deadly and complex tasks, ones that we humans couldn't have achieved alone."

They both looked at each other hard.

"Well Tony," he snapped with finality. "I think we've covered enough here. I'll leave you now. Get onto the street, and find this killer as soon as you can. As for the future of Takahashi Robotics and all the androids, well, that's for the authorities to decide. It's out of our jurisdiction. Our job, our goal here within the police department is just one... retire D4 with immediate effect! And you're the man to do it Tony. I'm counting on you!"

"Yes Sir, leave it with me...."

Tony drove his surface-vehicle slowly through New York City, his eyes scanning to and fro. It was buzzing with murmuring echoes, alive with sound. Further ahead, an autonomous truck rumbled. The self-driving robotic truck was collecting debris, cleaning city roads meticulously, efficiently. It sensed its environment with human-like awareness and moved safely. Then, to his right, he saw some humans dressed in bright yellow overalls, making vital street repairs. They activated the turbo-drills as he passed and the sound was almost deafening. Above, thick cloud covered the eerie skyline concealing any sight of the sun. Droplets of rain beat against the windscreen.

A sudden thought then came to him. *'Perhaps I should go visit Professor Hiroshi Takahashi, the Director of Takahashi Robotics. He's the main designer and maker of these androids. He will undoubtedly have some important information.'* He reflected on this for a short time, and then decided that this would be a good idea. However, he knew that it could turn out to be a heated discussion, given that the android D4 was killing, and that Hiroshi and his team of computer scientists were responsible for building it... He took a sharp left, seconds later, a sharp right, and was on his way...

Tony sat inside a large room in the main building of Takahashi Robotics. Pinned across the walls were a series of detailed charts showing how the androids were built and designed. He glanced at the ticking clock on the wall, and read the hour. Suddenly the door opened and Hiroshi Takahashi came walking in, sipping a tall glass of rum which was heavily iced. He was Japanese, and was dressed in a white lab coat.

"Greetings Detective Fletcher, it's nice to meet you. I'm Hiroshi. My assistant told me that you wanted to speak to me."

His English held the remnant of an accent. Hiroshi dropped into a chair facing him, and placed the rum on a small desk, the cubes of ice slowly fading into the cold liquid. Outside the sky was illuminated by white light accompanied by the cracking sound of thunder. He pulled out a cigarette, lit up, and started to smoke. A nimbus of grey smoke circled above his head.

"Hope you don't mind?"

"No, not at all," replied Tony.

"So, why have you come to see me, detective Fletcher? Is it to do with android D4?"

"Yes I'm the detective responsible for tracking down D4 and retiring it! You and your team here built it, thus know it better than anyone else."

"Yes, indeed..."

They held each other's gaze, the seconds ticking away. Hiroshi broke the silence.

"Tell me detective. How did you discover that D4 is the killer?"

"Come on Professor, you of all people should know... a bit of logic here. We know that it's D4 because we have caught it on camera during seven of the killings. Only three out of the ten were not caught on camera! We studied the films, magnified the image, and read the serial number engraved on its forehead which as you know, is distinct. It's D4...!"

"Indeed detective..." replied Hiroshi calmly.

"Professor, it's quite extraordinary what you and your team have created. The science and engineering that goes into building these programmed androids, these machines, is simply remarkable. But one of those machines that you built here, D4, has now turned violent and has been killing innocent people, ten in total. So my question is, why do you think this is happening, why is it not following the standard laws of robotics like all the others?"

"Well first, let me tell you a little bit about the androids that we build here, a brief, overall summary. All our androids are programmed, and were built with the intention of helping humans, helping our society within different domains. Our vision of the future was this: humans and robots working together. And the best way to achieve this was to build a robot with unscripted personality, that is, robot personality is set up in such a way that it can reason about what you have said to it, and then determine its own response via information space. It was built in such a way that it can access the different conversations it's had and think about them accordingly. In terms of aesthetics, developing facial expression within the world of AI, well, I simply analysed the physics of human facial expressions. Liquid is critical in human facial expression. Thus, we here at Takahashi Robotics developed a material that is based on the same physics as human facial expression material... a lipid bilayer, a fat. Basically, cells self assemble. They are filled with fluid. As a result, it takes very little force to achieve facial expression, and its movement is very elastic and facial expressions naturally fall into place. You also need some mechanics to get the facial expressions to move correctly. With anchors that are embedded in the material in the right way, you can achieve this. Very few motors are required for facial expression in androids. They can express even the most subtle expressions."

"I see," said Tony with intrigue, rubbing his jaw. "But to be honest Professor, facial expression in androids isn't really the issue here as interesting as this all is."

"In short detective," said Hiroshi, "my androids can process all sorts of information, facial recognition... voice recognition and so forth... Now, with regard to D4, well we here at Takahashi Robotics never expected such a dreadful thing to occur. As a whole, every robot built lives in harmony with man, adhering to the laws of robotics accordingly. We here at Takahashi Robotics believe D4 to be a freak occurrence, thus when you retire it, no more problems will ever arise. In short, this is a one-off freak incident which will not be repeated."

"But you can't guarantee that, can you?"

"Nothing in life is a guarantee detective. We work on probability here. And the probability of this occurring again is next to nothing, I can assure you. This is the reason why we are still in business. The authorities would have shut us down with immediate effect if they thought otherwise."

"Fine Professor, however, that still does not answer my initial question. Why do you think this is happening, why is it not following the standard laws of robotics like all the others?"

"Again, I must reiterate that it is a one-off freak incident, and it will not happen again. As to why this is happening, well, I'd say it was because there is some type of programming fault. At first, D4 was obeying the laws of robotics, it then suddenly changed and started killing! In short, it is a programming fault, nothing more; an algorithm defect."

"Okay," snapped Tony in exasperation. "If that's the case, if it all comes down to it being a programming fault, an algorithm defect, that in turn would suggest that you and your team of computer scientists here at Takahashi Robotics are indirectly responsible for ten deaths."

Hiroshi stood up, his face red with anger. "Detective Fletcher, every android that is built here has to go through meticulous tests before it is released into the world to engage with society. The authorities monitor these tests accordingly. Documents are then signed, and the robot is passed fit by the authorities. It goes through a vicious process, a chain of events before it is released into society, the world of humans. Thus, I object. Please leave. This discussion has come to an end."

Tony stood up, and said with an elaborated casualness, "I'm sorry if I offended you Professor. I'm used to thinking aloud but before I go, I want to leave you with this thought. What if computers, robots, androids are capable of somehow developing their own free will, their own thoughts over time? What if the brain, the nature of the mind whether biological or mechanical is subject to potential change... This is a worrying thought, don't you think?"

"Detective Fletcher, I've nothing more to say on the matter. Please leave...I sincerely hope you find D4 and retire it soon..."

"You can count on that Professor..."

Driving back through the city, Tony was caught in timeless frustration. Many hours had passed... Night had fallen. He circled the streets in a blur of thought, thinking about how he could find D4, clueless as to its whereabouts. It looked like an angel, but regardless, it wouldn't be easy to find amongst the masses. Sadly he came to the conclusion that he would have to catch it during a kill. That would mean another victim. '*How else*,' he thought? In order for him to catch it and retire it, it would have to kill again, and he would have to be somewhere close to the scene as it was happening.

He contemplated his discussion with Hiroshi at Takahashi Robotics. He wasn't happy with Hiroshi's reaction. He dwelt on the idea of androids, robots, developing their own free will. This filled him with dread and concern. He shook his head. The idea hooked his consciousness and dragged his mind into the harsh air of awareness... a potential reality...!

He drove on. Heavy rain began to fall, drenching the city with torrents of hot moisture. The city was densely populated; complex social interactions were taking place everywhere. It was a real mix of different cultures. He checked his wristwatch. Luminous dials shone in the gloom: It was 9pm. Glowing skyscrapers engulfed him from every angle. Endless numbers of people walked to and fro. Bars and restaurants were scattered all around, buzzing with perpetual activity. Sound filled the air; human voices commingling with city chaos. Bright neon signs flickered.

He adjusted the speed dial and the surface vehicle crept along the street at a safe controlled velocity with all the other vehicles. Sudden hunger gripped him; an avid hunger. He saw a drive-through burger-bar. He made a sharp right turn, signalling. The surface-vehicle moved slowly until he reached the open bar window. And there it halted. Instantly he smelt the scent of food. A young blonde woman stood there chewing gum.

"Howdy Sir," she muttered, with a smile that lit up her round dimpled face.

"What can I get you...?"

"Cheese burger," he replied returning the smile.

"That will be six-dollars please."

He pressed his finger against the steel credit-register which lay fixed by the open window. It bleeped, signalling a successful transaction. Behind the blonde waitress he recognized an android, a robot worker cleaning with brisk efficiency. The serial number D5 was engraved on its forehead. It had black hair, and dead inorganic black eyes. He could also see two humans, cooking, working away enthusiastically. Bits of muffled conversation drifted his way. Minutes passed. The blonde gave him the burger which lay in a soft container. He opened it and took a large bite. He ate rapidly, until it was consumed then tossed the empty plastic container into a nearby bin via the open window. He wiped his mouth then winked at the blonde.

"Hurry up," snapped a voice suddenly.

Behind, sitting in an elaborate sports car, was an impatient customer. He beeped his horn twice. The driver was listening to music, instrumental with a mystical Arabian beat. Tony drove away slowly, reconnecting with the flow of the main road. It was time to get home...

After ten minutes, he entered a quiet portion of the city. Above, in the atmosphere, the cold moon appeared and vanished almost rhythmically as dense red clouds of sulphuric acid passed it by. He gripped the wheel with both hands, hard tires splashing through the drenched city road. A passing spacecraft roared above in the atmosphere. Cold wind began to gain speed, surging like a raging tide. He studied himself in the steamy mirror above. Then, suddenly, he heard a shot, then the wail of a living being in terrible pain, followed by screaming. Chaos emerged. Alarmed, his heart raced. A man lay on the ground, motionless, dead...The few pockets of people that walked the street immediately congregated around the lifeless body that lay on the cold wet ground. Voices cried, echoing through the street. Tony looked on, and saw someone running into a side alley. '*It had to be D4, the android,*' he thought... the angel of death! It had to happen this way!

He slammed on the brakes, pulled over, opened the door, tumbled out and started to run. Instinctively he pulled out his bright-silver laser-gun and made his way down the alley. He sprinted hard through the thickening darkness, splashing into dirty puddles of rain water. Burning adrenaline raced through his body. Grit crunched beneath his feet. He passed a resting pigeon that suddenly exploded into flight battering its wings. Tony started to slow down, and finally halted in his tracks. He was still... staring, breathing deeply, fighting to catch his breath! He had reached a dead end, and there, standing before him, was the blond inorganic human-like android, D4 dressed in a green suit... the one and only killer machine, the angel of death. In the temporal silence their eyes locked; biological and mechanical eyes nailed together. Tony raised his laser-gun sharp-eyed, and said, "Why? Why did you kill all those innocent people?"

The android stood there silent, almost hidden in the darkness. It then replied with its humanoid voice, "I wanted to be human. And to be human means to kill..."

With that, Tony fired, retiring the android instantly... Suddenly, the intercom on his watch buzzed. It signalled for his immediate attention. He raised his arm. A face formed in the darkness in ripples of visual static; sophisticated digital mechanisms at work. It was his boss, James Grainger...

"Tony, where are you?"

"Job complete Sir, I've just retired D4."

"Great, but that's not the end of the problem, there's just been another murder. It was caught on camera, Android D5...!"